I'VE GOT MY
EYES ON YOU

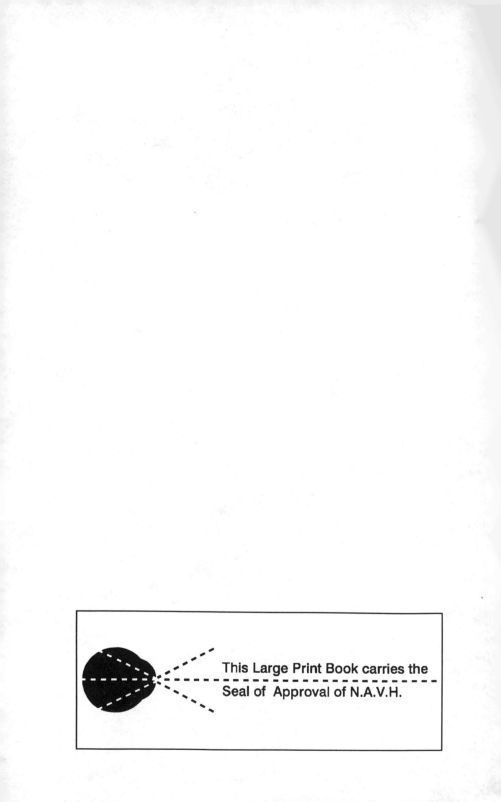

This Large Print Book carries the
Seal of Approval of N.A.V.H.

I'VE GOT MY EYES ON YOU

MARY HIGGINS CLARK

LARGE PRINT PRESS
A part of Gale, a Cengage Company

GALE
A Cengage Company

Farmington Hills, Mich • San Francisco • New York • Waterville, Maine
Meriden, Conn • Mason, Ohio • Chicago

LIBRARY OF CONGRESS CIP DATA ON FILE.
CATALOGUING IN PUBLICATION FOR THIS BOOK
IS AVAILABLE FROM THE LIBRARY OF CONGRESS.

ISBN-13: 978-1-4328-4799-9 (hardcover)
ISBN-13: 978-1-4328-4800-2 (paperback)

Published in 2019 by arrangement with Simon & Schuster, Inc.

Printed in the United States of America
1 2 3 4 5 6 7 23 22 21 20 19

For Elizabeth and Lauren
Wishing the two of you a
lifetime of happiness

ACKNOWLEDGMENTS

This newest book is finished. And it is time to thank all the people who shared their expertise and those who encouraged me along the way.

Michael Korda, my editor who for forty years has been my guiding light. All the thanks in the world, Michael.

Marysue Rucci, editor-in-chief of Simon & Schuster, who as always is a wise and discerning voice every step of the way.

John Conheeney, spouse extraordinaire, who for over twenty years has listened to me as I sigh that I am sure this book isn't working.

Kevin Wilder for all his help educating me on how a detective investigates a murder case.

Kelly Oberle-Tweed for giving me insight into the role of guidance counselors.

Mike Dahlgren for his advice on what a college would do if it had a controversial student headed its way.

My son Dave, who works with me every step of the way. Much of the credit for this plot belongs to him.

My grandson David, who has Fragile X syndrome. Thank you for inspiring my Jamie character.

Finally, and of course, to all of you, my readers, I hope I will entertain you in the time you give to reading this book. God bless you, one and all.

1

Jamie was in his room on the second floor of his mother's small Cape Cod house in Saddle River, New Jersey, when his life changed.

For a while he had been looking out the window to watch Kerry Dowling's backyard. She was having a party and Jamie was mad because she hadn't invited him. When they were in high school together, she was always nice to him even though he was in special classes. But Mom had told him that it was probably just a party only for Kerry's classmates who would be leaving for college next week. Jamie had graduated from high school two years ago and now had a good job stocking shelves in the local Acme supermarket.

Jamie didn't tell Mom that if the kids at the party started swimming in Kerry's pool, he was going to go over and swim with them. He knew Mom would be mad at him if he did that. But Kerry always invited him to swim in her pool when she was swimming. He watched from the window of his room until all the kids went home and Kerry was alone outside on the patio cleaning up.

He watched the end of his video. He decided to go over and help her, even though he knew Mom would not want him to.

He slipped downstairs, where Mom was watching the eleven o'clock news, and tiptoed behind the hedges that separated his small backyard from Kerry's big one.

But then he saw someone come into the yard from the woods. He grabbed something off a chair and came up behind Kerry, hit her on the head, and pushed her into the pool. Then he threw something away.

You're not supposed to hit people or push them in pools, Jamie thought. The man should say he's sorry, or he might get a time-out. Kerry's swimming, so I can go swimming with her, he told himself.

The man didn't go swimming. He ran away from the yard and back into the woods. He didn't go in the house. He just ran away.

Jamie hurried toward the pool. His foot kicked something that was on the ground.

It was a golf club. He picked it up, carried it toward the pool and put it on one of the chairs.

He said, "Kerry, it's Jamie. I'll go swimming with you now."

But she didn't answer him. He started to walk down the pool steps. The water looked dirty. He thought maybe somebody spilled something. But when he felt the water in his new sneakers, soaking his pants up to his knees, he stopped. Even though Kerry always said he could swim with her, he knew that Mom would be mad if he got his new sneakers wet. Kerry was floating in the water. He reached out, touched her shoulder and said, "Kerry, wake up." But Kerry just floated farther away, to the deep end of the pool. So he went back home.

The news was still on the television, so Mom didn't see him when he sneaked back upstairs and went to bed. He knew his sneakers, socks and pants were wet, so he hid them on the floor of his closet. Maybe they'll dry before Mom finds them, he hoped.

As he was falling asleep, he wondered if Kerry was having fun swimming.

2

It was after midnight when Marge Chapman woke up and realized that she had fallen asleep while she was watching the news. She got up slowly, her arthritic knees creaking as she pulled herself up from her big, comfortable chair. Jamie had been born when she was forty-five, and that was when she started putting on weight. I need to lose twenty-five pounds, she thought to herself, if only to give my knees a break.

She turned off the lights in the living room, then went upstairs to look into Jamie's room before she went to bed. His light was out and she could hear his even breathing so she knew he was asleep.

She hoped he hadn't been upset about not being invited to the party, but there was only so much she could do to protect him from disappointment.

3

At quarter to eleven on Sunday morning Steve and Fran Dowling crossed the George Washington Bridge and headed to their home in Saddle River, New Jersey, in silence. Both were tired from their long day on Saturday. Friends from Wellesley, Massachusetts, had invited them to a twenty-seven-hole member-guest golf tournament. They had stayed overnight, and this morning had left early to pick up their twenty-eight-year-old daughter, Aline, at Kennedy Airport and drive her home. Except for brief visits, she had been living abroad for three years.

After the joyous reunion at the airport, a jetlagged Aline had climbed into the backseat of the SUV and fallen asleep. Suppressing a yawn, Fran sighed, "Getting up so early two days in a row reminds me of my age."

Steve smiled. He was three months

younger than his wife, so she hit all the birthday milestones, in this case fifty-five, just before he did.

"I wonder if Kerry will be up when we get home," Fran said, as much to herself as to her husband.

"I'm sure she'll be at the front door waiting to welcome her sister," Steve replied, a smile in his voice.

Fran had her cell phone to her ear and listened as her call again went to Kerry's voicemail. "Our Sleeping Beauty is still in dreamland," she announced with a chuckle.

Steve laughed. He and Fran were both light sleepers. Their daughters were the opposite.

Fifteen minutes later they pulled into their driveway and woke up Aline. Still half-asleep, she stumbled into the house after them.

"Dear God," Fran exclaimed, as she looked around her usually tidy home. Empty plastic glasses and beer cans were on the coffee table and all over the living room. She walked into the kitchen to find an empty vodka bottle in the sink next to empty pizza boxes.

Completely awake now, Aline could tell her mother and father were upset and furious. She shared their feelings. Ten years older than her sister, she had an immediate sense that something was terribly wrong. If Kerry had a party, why didn't she have the brains to clean up afterward? Aline asked herself. Did she drink too much and pass out?

Aline listened as her mother and father hurried upstairs calling Kerry's name. They came back immediately.

"Kerry isn't here," Fran said, her voice now filled with concern. "And wherever she went, she didn't take her phone. It's on the table. Where is she?" Fran's face was becoming pale. "Maybe she got sick and someone took her home or —"

Steve interrupted her. "Let's start calling her friends. Someone is bound to know where she is."

"The lacrosse team roster with phone numbers is in the kitchen drawer," Fran said, as she began hurrying down the hallway. Kerry's closest friends were on the team.

Please let her be asleep at Nancy or Sinead's house, Aline thought. She must have been in really bad shape if she forgot to bring her cell phone with her. At least I can start to straighten up. She went into the kitchen. Her mother was starting to dial as her father read her a phone number. Aline grabbed a large garbage bag from the cabinet.

She decided to see if there was any junk on the back porch or the patio and pool area, and headed there.

What she saw on the porch startled her. A half-filled garbage bag on one of the chairs. When she glanced inside, she saw that it was stuffed with soiled paper plates, a pizza box and plastic cups.

Obviously Kerry had started to clean up. But why would she have stopped?

Uncertain about whether or not to tell her parents what she had found or to just let them keep making calls, Aline went down the four steps to the patio and walked over to the pool. It had been open all summer and she was looking forward to relaxing with Kerry in it before Kerry left for college and she began her new job as a guidance counselor at Saddle River High School.

The putter her parents would use to practice was lying across a chaise lounge on the pool deck.

Aline leaned over to pick up the putter and looked down in horror. Her sister was lying at the bottom of the pool, fully dressed and absolutely motionless.

4

Jamie loved to sleep late. He worked at the supermarket from eleven until three o'clock. Marge had his breakfast ready at ten o'clock. When he was finished, she reminded him to go upstairs and brush his teeth. Jamie came back, gave her a wide smile and waited for her to say, "Very nice," before he bolted out the door to go to "my job," as he proudly referred to it. It was a twenty-minute walk to Acme. As she watched him head down the block, Marge was aware that something was nagging at the back of her mind.

When she went upstairs to make his bed, she remembered what it was. Jamie was wearing his old scuffed sneakers, not the new ones she had bought for him last week. What on earth made him do that? she asked herself as she began to tidy up his room. And where are the new sneakers?

She walked over to his bathroom. He had

showered, and the towels and washcloth were in the hamper just where she had taught him to put them. But there was no sign of the new sneakers or the pants he had worn yesterday.

He wouldn't throw them away, she told herself, as she went back to Jamie's room and looked around. It was with both relief and dismay that she picked up his tangled belongings where he had left them on the floor of his closet.

The socks and sneakers were soaking wet. So was the lower half of his pants.

Marge was still holding them when she heard a piercing scream from the backyard. She ran to the window to see Aline leaping into the pool and her parents rushing out from the house.

She watched as Steve Dowling jumped into the pool next to Aline and came up carrying Kerry with Aline steps behind him. Horrified, Marge watched as he laid Kerry down and started pounding on her chest, shouting, "Call an ambulance!" In a matter of minutes, police cars and an ambulance were racing up the driveway.

Then Marge saw a policeman pull Steve away from Kerry as the crew from the ambulance knelt beside her.

Marge turned away from the window

when she saw the officer get back on his feet and start shaking his head.

It took a long minute before she realized she was still holding Jamie's pants, socks and sneakers. She knew without being told how they had gotten wet. Why would he have started to go down the steps to the pool and then come back out? And what are these stains?

She had to throw the pants, socks and sneakers in the washer and dryer immediately.

Marge didn't know why every bone in her body was screaming at her to do that, but without understanding why, she understood that she was protecting Jamie.

The wail of the police and ambulance sirens had drawn the neighbors out of their homes. The word spread quickly. "Kerry Dowling drowned in her pool." Many of the neighbors, some with coffee cups in their hands, hurried to the back of Marge's yard where they could see what was happening.

Marge's neighbors lived in the bigger houses surrounding her modest home. Thirty years ago she and Jack had bought their small Cape Cod on this curving, heavily treed property. Their neighbors had been like them, hardworking people in similar homes. Over the last twenty years the neighborhood had gone upscale. One by one the neighbors had sold their small homes to developers for double their value. Marge was the only one who had decided to stay. Now she was surrounded by more expensive homes, and the people who lived in them — doctors, lawyers and Wall Street businessmen — were all well-to-do. They were all pleasant to her, but it wasn't like the old days when she and Jack had been good friends with their neighbors.

Marge joined her neighbors and listened as some said they had heard the music from the party and seen a number of cars parked in the driveway and on the block. But they agreed that the kids who had gone to the party hadn't been very noisy and were all gone by eleven o'clock.

Marge slipped away back to her house.

I can't talk to anyone now, she thought. I need time to think, she said to herself. The clunk-clunk sound of Jamie's sneakers in the washing machine made her even more frantic.

She left the house for the garage, then pushed the button to open the garage door and backed out of her driveway. Careful to avoid making eye contact with any of her neighbors, she pulled away from the crowd of people gathered in her backyard and the increasing number of police who were on the patio and in the yard behind the Dowling home.

5

When Steve pulled Kerry's body out of the water, he laid her on the ground, frantically tried to resuscitate her and shouted to Aline to dial 911. He continued to try to force Kerry to breathe, stopping only when the first police car arrived and an officer pushed him aside and took over.

Agonizing and praying, Steve, Fran and Aline watched as the police officer knelt over Kerry, continuing to administer CPR.

Less than a minute later an ambulance came screeching up the driveway and paramedics jumped out. Steve, Fran and Aline looked on as one of them knelt over Kerry to take over the CPR. Her lips were closed and her slender arms extended away from her chest. The red cotton sundress was crumpled and soaking wet on her body. They stared down at Kerry unbelieving. Her hair was still dripping down on her shoulders.

"It would be easier for all of you if you went inside," they were told by one of the police officers. Silently Aline and her parents walked toward the house. They went inside and huddled at the window.

Working swiftly, the paramedics attached leads to Kerry's chest to transmit her vitals to the local emergency room at Valley Hospital. The attending physician quickly confirmed what everyone at the scene already believed. "Flatlined."

The medic who had taken over the CPR application noticed a trace amount of blood on Kerry's neck. Following his suspicion he lifted her head and saw a gaping wound at the base of her skull.

He showed it to the police officer in charge at the scene, who promptly called the Prosecutor's Office.

6

Homicide detective Michael Wilson, of the Bergen County Prosecutor's Office, was on call that day. He was settled with the newspapers on a chaise lounge at his condominium complex's swimming pool in Washington Township. Just starting to doze, he was startled by the ring of his cell phone, but quickly became alert. He listened as he was given his next case. "Teenage girl found dead in swimming pool at 123 Werimus Pines Road in Saddle River. Parents were away when she drowned. Local police report signs of a party at the property. Unexplained head trauma."

Saddle River borders Washington Township, he thought. I can drive there in ten minutes. He got up and started walking back to his unit, the feeling of chlorine on his skin. The first thing I'll do is shower. I might be working for the next two hours, twelve hours or twenty-four-plus hours straight.

He grabbed a freshly laundered long-sleeved sports shirt and khakis from his closet, tossed them on the bed and headed to the bathroom. Ten minutes later he was out of the shower, dressed and on his way to Saddle River.

Wilson knew that at the time he was called, the Prosecutor's Office also would have dispatched a photographer and a medical examiner to the scene. They would arrive shortly after him.

Saddle River, a borough of just over three thousand residents, was one of the very wealthy communities in the United States. Despite being surrounded by densely populated suburbs, a bucolic atmosphere pervaded the town. Its minimum two-acre zoning for homes and easy access to New York City made it a favorite of Wall Street titans and sports celebrities. Former President Richard Nixon owned a home there toward the end of his life.

Mike knew that as recently as the 1950s it had been a favorite site of local hunters. In the early days small ranch houses were built. Almost all of these were later replaced by much larger, more expensive homes, including its share of McMansions.

The Dowling home was a handsome

cream-colored Colonial with light green shutters. A cop was on duty on the street in front of the house and had cleared an area for official parking. Mike chose a spot and walked across the lawn to the back of the house. Spotting a group of Saddle River police officers, he asked who had been the first to respond. Officer Jerome Weld, the front of his uniform still wet, stepped forward.

Weld explained that he had arrived at the scene at 11:43 A.M. The family members had already pulled the body from the water. Although he was certain it was too late, he applied CPR. The victim was unresponsive.

He and other officers had conducted a preliminary search of the property. Clearly, there had been a gathering at the home the previous evening. Neighbors confirmed that they'd heard music coming from the Dowling home and observed a large number of young people entering and exiting the house and walking to and from their cars. In total some twenty to twenty-five vehicles had been parked on the street during the party.

The officer continued. "I called your office after I observed the gash on the back of the victim's head. When searching the property, we found a golf club by the pool that appears to have hair and blood on it."

Mike walked over, bent down and studied it carefully. As the cop had told him, there were several long, bloodstained hairs sticking to the putter head and drops of blood spattered on the shaft.

"Bag it," Mike said, "and we'll send it out for analysis."

As Mike was talking to the officer, the investigator from the Medical Examiner's Office arrived. Sharon Reynolds had worked several homicide cases with Mike. He introduced her to Officer Weld, who briefly summarized what they had found at the scene.

Reynolds knelt next to the body and began taking photographs. She slid the dress Kerry was wearing up to her neck to check for stab or other wounds and then examined her legs. Finding no injuries, she rolled the body over and continued to snap pictures. Moving Kerry's hair to the side, she photographed the deep gash at the base of her skull.

7

When Steve and Aline came back downstairs after changing their clothes, they joined Fran in the family room, which was still littered with plastic glasses and soiled paper plates. Officer Weld had instructed them not to clean up anything until the Prosecutor's Office arrived and had had an opportunity to examine both the outside property and the inside of the home.

Steve's arm was around Fran. They were sitting together motionless on the couch. Then Fran's voice began to shake and she exploded into high-pitched sobs.

They huddled together in mutual shock and overwhelming grief. "How could she have fallen into the pool fully dressed?" Fran wailed.

Steve said, "We know she was out on the patio cleaning up. Maybe she leaned over to get something that had fallen in the pool and then she fell. It was probably late and she may have been tired." He did not share with Fran or Aline his private fear that Kerry might have had way too much to drink.

Quietly tearful, Aline was thinking. Poor Kerry, poor baby. She had been in frequent contact with Kerry in the three years she had been away. She could not fathom that she would never see or hear from her again. She couldn't believe that yet again she was forced to deal with the sudden death of someone she loved.

Fran was quietly sobbing now.

There was a chiming from the doorbell, then the unlocked front door was pushed open. It was Monsignor Del Prete, "Father Frank" as he preferred to be called. The sixty-six-year-old pastor of St. Gabriel's, their local parish, came in. Obviously someone had phoned him, because he said at once, "Fran, Steve, Aline, I am so terribly sorry." As they stood up, he clasped each of their hands in his and then pulled up a chair close to them. He said quietly, "I would like to say a prayer for Kerry." He began, "Dear Lord, in this time of great sorrow . . ."

When he'd finished it, Fran burst out, "How could God do this to us?"

Father Frank took off his glasses, removed a smooth cloth from his pocket and began to clean them as he spoke. "Fran, that is a question everyone asks after a tragedy. How can our all-loving and merciful God fail to protect us and those we love at the time when we most need him? I'll be honest with you. It's a question I struggle with myself.

"The best answer I've heard came in a sermon given by an elderly priest many years ago. He was traveling in the Middle East and was overwhelmed by the majesty of the Persian rugs he saw. Those gorgeous creations so skillfully woven into such beautiful designs. One day he was in a shop where those rugs were on display. He walked behind one that was hanging on hooks from the ceiling. Looking at it from behind, he was shocked to behold a confusing array of threads that led nowhere. Such beauty on one side, total disharmony on the other, but both part of the same plan. It was then that the message became clear to him. In this life we see only the back side of the rug. We don't know how or why our unspeakable hardships are part of a beautiful design. That is why having faith is so important."

The silence that followed was broken by a knock on the back door. As Steve got up, there was the sound of footsteps coming down the hallway. A man in his early thirties, with sandy hair and piercing brown eyes stood before them. He introduced himself by saying, "My name is Detective Mike Wilson from the Bergen County Prosecutor's Office. I am so sorry for your loss. Would it be okay if I asked you a few questions? We need basic background information."

Father Frank got up and offered to stop back later.

Fran and Steve, speaking almost in unison, asked him to stay. He nodded and sat down again.

"What is your daughter's age?" the detective asked.

It was Aline who answered. "She was eighteen in January. She just graduated from high school."

The questions were gentle and easy to answer. Steve and Fran confirmed they were Kerry's parents and that Aline was her older sister.

"When was the last time you were in touch with your daughter in any way — phone, text, email?"

They agreed it was about five o'clock the previous evening. Steve explained that they had stayed overnight with friends in Massachusetts and gotten up early this morning to pick up Aline at Kennedy Airport. She was coming back from London.

"Are you aware that a party was being held in your home last evening?"

Of course, the answer was no.

"There is evidence that liquor was served at the party. Did your daughter drink alcohol or use drugs?"

Fran's no was indignant. "She certainly did not use drugs," Steve said. "I'm sure she had an occasional beer or glass of wine with her friends."

"We want to talk to her close friends. Can you give me their names?"

"Most of her close friends were on the high school lacrosse team," Steve said. "The roster is in the kitchen. I can get it for you." Then he added, "Is there any particular reason you want to speak to them?"

"Yes, there is. As far as we know, there were a lot of people in your home last night. We want to find out who they were and what went on at the party. Your daughter has a severe injury to the back of her head. We need to know what caused it."

"Could she have fallen and hit her head?"

"That is a possibility. It is also possible that Kerry was struck with an object. We'll know more after we receive the medical examiner's report."

Someone deliberately hit her over the head, Aline thought. They think she was murdered.

"There was a golf club on one of the chairs by the pool. There is evidence that it may have been used as a weapon."

It was Steve who asked quietly, "What are you trying to tell us?"

"Mr. and Mrs. Dowling," Wilson began, "we'll know more after we receive the results of the medical examination, but I am sorry to tell you we are treating your daughter's death as suspicious and will investigate it accordingly."

Still trying to absorb what she was hearing, Aline said, "I can't believe any of the kids she invited here last night would want to hurt her."

"I understand you feeling that way," Wilson said empathetically, "but we have to check out everything."

He paused. "Another question. Did she have a boyfriend, someone special?"

Fran spat out the answer. "Yes, she did. His name is Alan Crowley. He was very possessive of Kerry and he has a terrible temper. If anyone hurt my child, I'm sure he was the one."

Mike Wilson did not let his expression change. "Could I see that list now? I also want to know who were her closest friends."

"I can help you with that," Steve said quietly.

"And one more thing. We did not find a cell phone in your daughter's clothing. Do you know where it is, and would it be okay if we take it?"

"Of course. It's on the dining room table," Fran said.

"I have a consent form in my car. I'll ask you to sign it to allow me to take and examine the phone."

"The unlock code is 0112," Aline said as her eyes filled with tears. "The month of her birthday and then of mine."

Aline pulled out her phone and began tapping on it. "Detective Wilson, yesterday morning I received a text from Kerry: *I have something VERY IMPORTANT to talk to you about when you get home!!!*"

Wilson leaned forward. "Do you have any idea what she was referring to?"

"No, I'm sorry, I don't. Kerry could be a little dramatic. I just assumed it was boyfriend or college related."

"Aline, I might have to speak to you again as the investigation goes forward. Will you be returning to London?"

She shook her head. "No, I'm home for good. In fact I'm about to start a new job as a guidance counselor at Saddle River

High School."

Mike paused, then said gently to all of them, "I know how awful this is for you. I'm going to ask you to help me in a very important way. Don't share information with anyone about the wound on Kerry's head or our concern about the golf club. As we question others in the coming days and weeks, it is critical that as few details as possible be made public."

The Dowlings and Father Frank all nodded in agreement.

"I will talk to you again before I leave today. And please don't clean up anything until the investigators go through it and we determine if we need to take anything with us."

8

After returning to the house to have the consent form signed for Kerry's cell phone and laptop, Detective Wilson spoke to the officers who were conducting a search of the Dowling home and property. From there, in his car, he tapped in the cell phone's unlock code and hit the text messages icon. The first four were brief notes from girls thanking Kerry for the good time they had at the party. One said she hoped Kerry would be able to patch things up with Alan, while another advised her to dump "that jerk" and hoped Kerry was okay after the fight. Mike jotted down the names of the four girls as party attendees he would interview.

He then clicked on the text message trail from "Alan." He skipped to the bottom of the chain so he could read the messages in the order they were sent.

Alan at 10:30: *Hope you and Chris are*

enjoying yourselves. I'm at Nellie's. Felt like decking him. And you!

Kerry at 10:35: *Thanks for ruining my party. You made an ASS of yourself. You don't own me. I'll talk to whoever I want. Do me a favor. Get out of my life.*

Alan at 11:03: *Sorry I lost it. I wanna see you now. Bad enough Chris will be after you when you're both at BC. You didn't have to start tonite.* Mike wondered if "BC" meant "Boston College."

Kerry at 11:10: *Don't come over. Tired! Will finish cleaning backyard then going to sleep. Talk tomorrow.*

This is going to be a ground ball, Mike thought, using detective parlance for a case that would be easily solved. Jealous boyfriend. She's ready to move on. He isn't. At least one of her girlfriends telling her to end it.

Mike put down the phone. Using his dashboard computer, he accessed the Department of Motor Vehicles records. He typed in "Alan Crowley, Saddle River." A moment later Crowley's driver's license filled the screen.

His next call was to the captain in charge of the homicide unit at the Prosecutor's Office. He gave a summary of what he had found at the Dowling home and Kerry's altercation with her boyfriend at the party. "Ordinarily, I'd want to talk to the kids who were at the party before interviewing the boyfriend, but I'm worried that will give him a chance to lawyer up. He lives here in Saddle River. I'm five minutes away. My gut tells me I should go have a chat with him right now and lock him into a statement."

"You're sure he's not a minor?" the captain asked.

"His driver's license says he turned eighteen last month."

There was a pause. Mike knew that he should not interrupt his boss when he was thinking. Mike also knew that although Crowley was legally an adult, judges tended to give defendants latitude if they had only just turned eighteen.

"Okay, Mike. Call me after you talk to him."

The Crowley home was on heavily treed Twin Oaks Road. It was a very large, white, shingled house with dark green shutters. Very impressive, Mike thought. From what he could see of the beautifully landscaped front and side yards, it was easily more than two acres. Big bucks here, he decided. A riding mower was parked on the edge of the driveway.

Mike rang the doorbell. There was no immediate answer. He waited for a full minute before he rang it again.

Alan Crowley had been mowing the lawn and was hot. He had gone into the house for a bottle of water. He glanced at the cell phone he had left on the kitchen table and saw there were a number of voicemail messages, missed calls and texts. Carrying his phone as he walked to the door, he only needed to read one text before the reality of the nightmare that was enveloping him sunk in.

The doorbell rang again. Kerry was dead. The rumor is she was murdered. The cops are talking to the neighbors and asking if they knew the names of the kids who had been at the party last night. They're bound to find out he and Kerry had a fight.

Terrified, he went to the door and opened it.

The man at the door introduced himself while pointing to the badge on a chain around his neck. "I'm Detective Mike Wilson, Bergen County Prosecutor's Office," he said, his tone friendly. "Are you Alan Crowley?"

"Yes."

From the expression on the young man's face, Wilson was sure that he had heard that

Kerry was dead.

"Are you aware of what happened to Kerry Dowling?" he asked.

"You mean that Kerry is dead?"

"Yes. . . ."

"Why are you here?"

"I'm going to find out what happened to Kerry. I'm starting by talking to everyone who was at the party last night. Would it be okay if we chat for a little while?"

"Yeah, I guess so. Do you want to come in?"

"Alan, let's take a ride down to my office in Hackensack. We can talk there with no interruptions. You don't have to go, but it will make things a lot easier. Come on. I'll drive. Oh, Alan, before we go, do you remember what you were wearing at the party last night?"

"Yeah. Why?"

"Just procedure."

Alan thought for a moment. I'm better off cooperating than looking defensive. I've got nothing to worry about. "I had on a Princeton T-shirt, shorts and sandals."

"Where are they?"

"They're in my room."

"Would you mind putting them in a bag and letting me keep them for a few days? Routine procedure. You don't have to, but we would really appreciate your cooperation."

"Yeah, I guess so," Alan said reluctantly.

"I'll go with you," Mike said amicably.

Shorts, a T-shirt and a pair of underwear were the items at the top of the hamper. Alan put them in a small gym bag. He grabbed his sandals and put them in as well. Holding his cell phone in one hand and the gym bag in the other, he woodenly followed the detective out to his car.

Mike Wilson had no intention of interrogating Alan before they got to his office at the courthouse. He knew that the more he could put him at ease, the more Alan would say once the camera was recording.

"When I was at the Dowling property, Alan, I noticed a putting green. The Dowlings must really be into golf. Do you play?"

"I've gone to driving ranges and played a few rounds. I play baseball in the spring and summer so I really don't have much time for golf."

"When you were at Kerry's party, was anybody using the putting green?"

"I saw some guys fooling around on it last night. But I didn't use it."

"I noticed you wore a Princeton shirt to the party. Any significance in that?"

"Oh, yeah," Alan said while staring out the car window. "The day I found out I was accepted, my mother went on the school website and bought Princeton logo stuff for me and tennis clothes for her and my father. They were really excited about my getting in."

"That's a great accomplishment. Your parents and you should be very proud. Are you looking forward to college?"

"I'm looking forward to being on my own, Princeton or wherever."

Their conversation was interrupted when Mike's phone rang. After he answered, a voice came through the speaker. "Mike, we have a ninety-three-year-old male who was found dead in his Fort Lee apartment by a neighbor. No sign of forced entry."

Mike hit a button on his cell phone that took the call off speaker. He put the phone to his ear and listened.

Alan welcomed the interruption. He needed time to think. In his mind he meticulously reviewed every minute of his activities.

The fight with Kerry at the party was because Chris was hanging around her saying that he'd help her get settled in at Boston College. The *Felt like decking you* text he had sent her.

I went to Nellie's because I knew the guys would be there, he thought. Then I started to sober up. I wanted to make up, so I'll say I wanted to help her clean up. Kerry texted back that she was too tired to clean up. And I went back to her house anyhow.

His blood froze at the thought.

They think *I* killed Kerry. The detective will try to get me to admit it. His mind scurried around for answers. He came up with only one. The guys at Nellie's have to cover for me, Alan thought. If they'll say I was with them until 11:45, I'll be okay. I got home around midnight. Mom and Dad were home, and Mom yelled good night to me from their room. I drove fast. I made it home in less than ten minutes. I wouldn't have had time to go to Kerry's on the other side of town and get home that fast.

I'll tell the guys to say I was with them until they left Nellie's. They'll do it for me. That reassurance calmed Alan. He fought to stay calm as he was led into an interrogation room. The first questions were easy ones. How long had he and Kerry been friends?

"Kerry and I have been together for a year, I guess. Oh, sure, we have arguments. Sometimes Kerry starts them. She likes me to be jealous."

43

"Did you have an argument at the party?"

"Yeah, but it was really nothing. This guy Chris has been trying to get between us. He was all over Kerry at the party."

Wilson said, "I'll bet that got you really mad."

"It did at first, but I got over it. It's happened before, but we always end up okay. Like I said, Kerry likes to make me jealous."

As he answered the questions Wilson was asking, Alan thought, This isn't nearly as bad as I thought it would be.

"Alan, many people get angry when they're jealous. Do you?"

"Sometimes, but I get over it right away."

"Okay. What time did you leave the party?"

"Around ten-thirty."

"How long had you been at the party?"

"I got there about seven."

"Alan, it's important that you tell me. Did you have any drugs or alcohol before you got there or while you were at the party?"

"I never do drugs. There were no drugs at the party. I did have a couple of beers."

"Did anybody leave the party with you?"

"No, I was by myself in my car."

"Where did you go?"

"I drove ten minutes to Nellie's in Waldwick and had a pizza with some friends who were already there."

"Who were these friends?"

"Bobby Whalen, Rich Johnson and Stan Pierce, friends of mine from the baseball team."

"Had they also been at the party?"

"No."

"Had you planned to meet them at Nellie's?"

"No, but I knew they were going to a movie and then to Nellie's. I was pretty sure they'd be there."

"What time did you get to Nellie's?"

"About ten-forty."

"How long did you stay?"

"I ate and stayed with them for about an hour."

"What did you do then?"

"I left and drove straight home."

"Did your friends leave at the same time?"

"Yeah, we all walked out together."

"What time did you get home?"

"About midnight, maybe a little before that."

"Was anybody home?"

"Yeah, my mom and dad. They were watching TV in their bedroom. I yelled good night."

"Did they hear you come in?"

"Yeah, my mom yelled good night back to me."

"At any time after you left the party at ten-thirty, and before or after you went home, did you ever go back to Kerry's house?"

"No, definitely not."

"Did you call or text Kerry at any time after you left the party?"

"I didn't call her, but I sent her a text and she answered me."

"Was it about the argument?"

"Yeah, we were both kind of teed off."

Wilson did not pursue this further because he had already seen the text messages on Kerry's phone. He also knew that he would get a court order for any other messages or calls Alan had made.

"Alan, just a few more questions." Mike asked, "You have a cell phone, right?"

"Sure I do."

"You used your phone when you sent texts to Kerry last night, right?"

"Yeah, of course."

"What's the number?"

Alan reeled it off.

"So, Alan, you went to the party at Kerry's house, and then to Nellie's, and then straight home. Did you have your cell phone with you that whole time?"

"Yeah, I did."

"Alan, the Dowlings have a putting green in their backyard. Did you see anybody using it at the party?"

"Like I told you before, some of the guys were on the putting green."

"Do you remember if you used it at any time last night?"

"I never went over to the practice green. No."

"So you never touched the putter last night?"

"No."

"Alan, it was warm last night. Did anyone go swimming in the pool?"

"No, not while I was there."

"Did you go in the pool?"

"No."

"Alan, while you're here, I have a request that will save us some time later. There are a lot of objects at Kerry's house that have fingerprints on them. I'd like to know whose fingerprints are on which objects. Would you consent to being fingerprinted before you leave? You don't have to, but it will be very helpful to us."

Fingerprinted, Alan thought to himself. They must believe I did it. The interrogation room suddenly felt smaller. Was the door locked? Why did I agree to come here?

Alan was trying desperately not to show his panic, but he was afraid to refuse. "I guess that would be okay," he said.

"And finally Alan, we'd like to take a swab of saliva from inside your cheek. That will give us your DNA. Any problem with that?"

"Okay." Numbly he followed Wilson into another room where his fingerprints were scanned and the swab taken.

"Alan, I appreciate how cooperative you've been. I have one final request. Would you mind leaving your cell phone with me for a few days?"

Thoroughly frightened, Alan pulled it from his pocket and placed it on the table. "Okay, but I want to go home now."

They did not exchange a word during the twenty-minute ride back to Saddle River.

9

The minute Wilson dropped him off, Alan rushed into his house. His parents had not yet returned from golf. He ran to the landline in the living room and paused for a moment as he groped for Rich's number. Rich answered on the first ring.

"Rich, this is Alan. Where are Stan and Bobby?"

"They're here at the pool with me."

"Listen, a detective had me go down to his office at the courthouse. He kept asking about my fight with Kerry. I told him that I stayed with you guys at Nellie's until we all left together. You got to promise you'll back me up. Otherwise, they'll think I killed Kerry. You know I would never hurt her. You know that. Ask the other guys now."

"They can hear you. I have it on speaker."

"Rich, ask them. Ask them."

As he held the phone, Alan could hear his three friends say, "Sure, I will. We're with you. Don't worry."

"Thanks guys. I knew I could count on you."

Alan hung up the phone and burst into sobs.

After the call Bobby, Rich and Stan looked at one another. All three of them were reviewing exactly what happened last night. They still had a hard time believing that Kerry was dead.

Like Alan, they would be leaving soon for college. They had gone to a movie and afterward went to Nellie's for pizza.

They were there at 10:45 P.M. when Alan had stomped in. All they needed to do was look at his face to know he was angry. He pulled up a chair at the table where they were sitting and signaled to the waitress, pointing at the individual pizzas at the table and indicating he wanted a plain one.

It was clear to the others that he had been drinking. Rich asked if he had taken an Uber to Nellie's.

Alan's slurred response was "No, I'm fine."

The bigger room by this time was mostly empty. The crowd in the bar area where they were sitting had gathered to watch the Yankees. The game against Boston was in extra innings. The shouts and clapping made the room noisy enough to prevent their conversation from being heard at neighboring tables.

Stan was the first to speak. "Alan, it's pretty obvious you've been drinking a lot. This is a popular hangout for cops. The Waldwick police station is right around the corner."

"Don't worry about me," Alan snarled. "I got here okay; I'll get home okay."

"What's eating you?" Bobby asked, annoyed at Alan's tone. "It's not even eleven. How was Kerry's party? Is it over already?"

"It sucked," Alan said. "I walked out. That jerk Chris Kobel was hanging all over Kerry. I told him to leave and Kerry started in on me."

"She'll get over it," Bobby said. "You two are always fighting and making up."

"Not this time. Right in front of me, Chris was telling her they should try to arrive at BC at the same time so he can help her move in. He's moving in on her and didn't care if I heard him."

Before the other three could comment, Alan heard a ping from his cell phone signaling that he had received a text. He reached into his shirt, pulled out his phone and quickly read a message. It was from

Kerry. Using two fingers, he typed a response.

The waitress came over with his steaming pizza and Alan asked for a Coke. As he devoured the slices and sipped his drink, it was obvious he was calming down and sobering up. The other three sensed that the exchange of texts had toned down the argument. They started following the Yankee game more closely when each team hit three-run home runs in the twelfth inning.

After fifteen minutes Alan pushed back his chair. "Kerry said everybody had to be out by eleven o'clock. It's twenty past. I'm going to swing by her house and straighten things out."

"Fine," Bobby said.

"Good luck," Stan added.

"Are you sure you're okay driving?" Rich asked. "Why don't you stay and watch the game?"

"I'm *fine,*" Alan said in a voice that made it clear the conversation was over.

A minute later the waitress came over with Alan's check. Not seeing him, she asked, "Is one of you taking care of this?"

"Give it to me," Rich said. "I'll collect from him tomorrow. Assuming he remembers he came here tonight."

Twenty minutes later the Yankees scored

the winning run and they decided it was time to call it quits. They piled into Stan's car and he dropped them off at their homes.

10

It was much too early to pick up Jamie at his job. Instead Marge slipped into a pew at St. Gabriel's church and began to pray. At two-thirty she drove to the Acme parking lot and managed to find a spot where she could see him the minute he left the store.

She spent that half hour in continued prayer. "Dear merciful Blessed Mother, please help the Dowlings find a way to cope with their tragedy. And *please,* don't let it be that Jamie had something to do with it. Jack, if only you were here to help us. He needs you." It was a prayer she had made to her husband over the five years since he had his fatal heart attack.

"Dear God, You know he would never hurt anyone. But if he thought he was just playing, and he's so strong — please —"

An image of Jamie holding Kerry underwater haunted Marge's mind. Suppose Jamie saw her in the pool and started to go down the steps. Maybe when she was swimming near him, he reached down to grab her. They used to play a game — who could stay underwater longer? Suppose he held her under until she was — ?

Marge's agonized thinking was broken only by the sight of Jamie coming out of the store holding two heavy grocery bags in each hand. She watched as he followed an older woman to her car. Jamie waited while she used her key to pop open the trunk. He hoisted up the bulging plastic bags and placed them gently into her trunk. He is so strong, Marge thought with a shudder.

Jamie closed the trunk and started across the parking lot. He walked over to a waiting limo and shook hands with his coworker Tony Carter, who was opening the door and stepping into the backseat. Marge heard Jamie yell "Have fun!" as the SUV pulled away.

A delighted smile came over his face when he saw her. Waving the way he always did, with his palm pushed forward and his fingers back, he walked over to the car, opened the door and got in beside her.

"Mom, you came to pick me up," he announced, his voice triumphant.

Marge leaned over and kissed her son as she smoothed back the sandy hair on his forehead.

But Jamie's happy smile quickly evaporated, and his voice became very serious. "Mom, are you mad at me?"

"Why would I be mad at you, Jamie?"

For a long moment a troubled look came over his face. That moment gave Marge time to look at him and, as always, realize what a handsome young man he was.

Jamie has Jack's blue eyes and even features, his six-foot height and perfect posture. The only difference was that Jamie had been deprived of oxygen during a difficult birth, and it had damaged his brain.

She could see that he was trying to remember why she might have been upset with him.

"My sneakers and socks and jeans got wet," he said haltingly. "I'm sorry. Okay?"

"How did they get wet, Jamie?" Marge asked, trying to sound matter-of-fact as she waited before turning the key to start the car.

Jamie's eyes were pleading. "Don't be mad at me, Mom."

"Oh, Jamie," Marge said quickly, "I'm not mad at you. But I just need for you to tell me what happened when you went over to Kerry's pool."

"Kerry was swimming," Jamie said while

looking down.

She was fully dressed, Marge thought. I saw her when Steve carried her out of the pool.

"Did you see her swimming in her pool?"

"Yes, she went swimming," he said, not making eye contact with his mother.

She may have been still alive when he saw her, Marge thought to herself. "Jamie, did you ask Kerry if you could go swimming with her?"

"Yes, I did."

"What did she say to you?"

Jamie looked straight ahead, trying to reconstruct in his mind a picture of the previous evening. "She said, 'Jamie, you can always go swimming with me.' I said, 'Thank you, Kerry. You're very nice.' "

Marge sighed inwardly. Time was always a hazy concept for Jamie. A memory of a place they visited a week ago would intertwine with his recollections of visiting that same place years earlier. Did this conversation with Kerry take place last night or on one of the many previous times she had invited him to swim with her?

"Jamie, why did you go swimming with your pants and sneakers on?"

"I'm sorry, Mom. I won't do it again. I promise, okay?" Jamie said, his voice growing louder and aggressive.

"Jamie, did you and Kerry play any games in the pool?"

"Kerry went under the water for a long time. I said, 'Kerry, wake up. It's Jamie.' "

"Did you help Kerry in the water?"

"I always help Kerry. I'm her friend."

"When you were playing a game, did you hold Kerry under the water?"

"I said I was sorry, Mom, okay?" Jamie said, as he started to tear up. "I want to go now."

"It's all right, Jamie," Marge said, as it was obvious that Jamie was beginning to shut down. But she had to figure out a way to protect him.

"Jamie," she said, trying to make her voice sound cheerful, "can you keep a secret?"

"I like secrets," Jamie said, "like birthday presents."

"That's right, like when we buy somebody a birthday present, we keep it a secret," Marge said. "But this secret will be about your going swimming with Kerry last night. Can that be a secret for only you and me?"

While using his finger to make a big X on his chest, Jamie said, "Cross my heart and hope to die," as he smiled widely.

Marge sighed. That would have to do for

now. "Do you want to come home with me, Jamie?"

"Can I watch practice?"

Marge knew he meant the football, soccer or whatever team was on the field at the high school. "Yes, you can. I'll drop you off. Be sure to come straight home afterwards."

"I will, Mom, and I won't tell anybody I was in the pool."

As if he was trying to change the subject, Jamie said, "Tony Carter and his dad are going on a fishing trip."

I hope they catch nothing but colds, Marge thought. She had heard that Carl Carter had told people that the only problem with Jamie was that "he didn't have his head screwed on tight." It was a remark that Marge neither forgave nor forgot. "That's nice," she managed to say.

As his mother drove, Jamie looked out the window at the passing houses. It's a secret, he told himself. I won't tell anybody I went swimming with Kerry. I won't tell anybody I got my sneakers, pants and socks wet, and I won't tell anybody about Big Guy who hit Kerry and pushed her in the pool. Because that's a secret too.

11

The instant he pulled into his driveway, Doug Crowley became irritated. "I told Alan the lawn should be mowed by the time we got home. Look! The front is only half-finished."

The consternation on June's face matched her husband's. Their avid tennis playing kept them in good shape. Both were on the short side. Doug was five feet, nine inches tall, with salt and pepper hair combed over to cover a growing bald spot. His even features always hinted at a scowl. June's cap-length brown hair did not do enough to soften her narrow lips and frequent frown.

June and Doug had been thirty-three years old when they married. By then June had her nursing degree from Rutgers and Doug was working as a software engineer. They were joined at the hip by their mutual desire to have a beautiful home, become members of a country club and retire by age sixty.

They were goal-oriented and insisted their only child be the same way.

To arrive home and find a job not completed and the mower sitting in the middle of the front lawn irritated June as much as it did Doug. She was fresh on her husband's heels when they went through the door shouting their son's name. When he did not answer, they went through the rooms and found him lying atop his unmade bed, crying. As one they began to shake him.

"Alan, what happened? What's the matter?"

At first Alan could not answer. Finally he looked up at them. "Kerry was found dead in her pool, and the police think I did it."

Doug was practically shouting, "Why do they think you did it?"

"Because we had an argument at her party. It was in front of a lot of the other kids. And when the detective was here, he —"

"A detective came here!" June shrieked. "Did you talk to him?"

"Yes. For a little while. He drove me to his office and asked me some questions."

Doug looked at his wife. "Did the detective have a right to do that?"

"I don't know. He did turn eighteen last month." She looked at her son. "Alan, exactly what happened to Kerry?"

His voice halting, Alan told them what he had learned. Kerry had been found in her pool this morning. "They think somebody hit her over the head and pushed her in and she drowned."

It ran through June's mind to tell Alan that they knew how much he had cared about Kerry. There would be time for that later. Right now, the tremendous impact of what they had heard and how it might affect Alan made it absolutely necessary to protect her son any way she could.

As she questioned him, she became more and more frantic.

12

After dropping Jamie at the high school, Marge drove down the block toward her home. Grace, her next-door neighbor, was watching for her from the patio on her front lawn. As soon as Marge parked the car, Grace waved her over.

"Can you believe it? That poor girl, Kerry, was murdered. She had one of those teen parties the kids have when their parents are away. The police are talking to all the neighbors. They rang your doorbell. They asked me if I knew who lived in your house. I told them about you and Jamie and said I didn't know where you were."

Marge tried to conceal her anxiety.

"Grace, did you say anything about Jamie?"

"I told them that he is a very nice young man with special needs and didn't go to the high school anymore. I guess they want to talk to everybody in the neighborhood who might have seen something."

"I suppose so," Marge agreed. "I'll see you later."

When Jamie came home a few hours later, Marge could see that something was disturbing him. She didn't have to ask him what it was before he said, "The girls on the soccer team were sad because Kerry went to Heaven."

"Jamie, a policeman is going to come and talk to us about Kerry because she got sick in the pool and went to Heaven. Remember you won't tell him that you went over to the pool."

The words were barely out of her mouth before the bell rang. Jamie started up the stairs to his room. When Marge answered the door, it was not a policeman in uniform but a man in a suit.

"I'm Detective Mike Wilson from the Bergen County Prosecutor's Office," he said.

"Yes, come in, Detective," Marge said, as she gestured toward the living room. "We can sit in here and talk."

After they settled into two chairs facing each other, Mike said, "As I'm sure you are aware, Mrs. Chapman, your neighbor Kerry Dowling was found dead in her family's swimming pool this morning."

"I did hear about it," Marge sighed. "A

terrible tragedy. Such a lovely young girl."

"Mrs. Chapman, my understanding is that you and your son live in this home?"

"Yes, just the two of us."

"Were the two of you home last night after eleven o'clock?"

"Yes, we both were."

"Was anyone else with you?"

"No, just us."

"Let me tell you why I am particularly interested in speaking to you and your son. When I was called to the Dowlings' home this morning, I stood at their backyard pool and looked around. Above the tree level I could clearly see the upstairs room in the back of your home. That means anyone who was in that room might have seen something that could be helpful to our investigation."

"Of course," Marge said.

"I'd like to see that room before I leave. How is that room used?"

"It's a bedroom."

"Your bedroom?"

"No, it's Jamie's bedroom."

"May I speak to him?"

"Of course."

Marge walked over to the stairs and called up to Jamie.

Detective Wilson interrupted her. "If it's okay with you, Mrs. Chapman, can I talk to

Jamie in his room?"

"I guess that would be okay," Marge said as she began to climb the stairs with the detective one step behind her. She knocked tentatively on Jamie's door and then opened it. He was sprawled on his bed watching a video.

"Jamie, I want you to meet Detective Wilson."

"Hi Jamie," Mike said, extending his hand forward.

Jamie stood up. "I'm pleased to meet you, sir," he said as he shook hands. He turned to Marge for her approval. Her smile confirmed to him that he had used good manners.

Jamie and Marge sat on the bed. Mike went over to the window. The Dowlings and the Chapmans were backyard neighbors. He looked down at the Dowling swimming pool, then sat in the chair opposite the bed.

"Jamie, I just want to talk to you for a few minutes. You know Kerry Dowling, don't you?"

"Yes. She's in Heaven."

Wilson smiled. "That's right, Jamie. She went to Heaven. But her parents and the police want to find out what happened before she went to Heaven. There was a party last night at Kerry's house."

66

"Kerry didn't invite me."

"I know you weren't there, Jamie, I just —"

"It was for the kids who just graduated. I'm older. I'm twenty years old. I just had my birthday."

"Well, happy birthday, Jamie." Wilson went over to the window. "Jamie, I can see Kerry's backyard and pool from here. So that means if you were in your room last night, you could too."

"I didn't go swimming with Kerry," Jamie said as he looked at his mother with a conspiratorial smile.

Mike smiled. "I know you didn't, Jamie. Did you see Kerry in her backyard cleaning up last night?"

"I help clean up at the Acme, where I work from eleven o'clock to three o'clock."

"So you didn't see Kerry in her backyard or see her go into her pool last night?"

"I did not go swimming with Kerry. I promise," Jamie said as he put his arm around his mother and kissed her.

"Okay. Thank you Jamie. Mrs. Chapman, I'm going to leave you my card. Sometimes people recall things later. If you or Jamie think of anything that might be helpful to our investigation, please contact me."

They walked downstairs and accompanied

Wilson to the front door. After Marge closed it behind him, Jamie gave her a triumphant smile and exclaimed, "I kept the secret!"

Marge put her finger to her lips and uttered "Shhhhhhh." She was terrified that the detective might have lingered on the porch and heard Jamie. Heart in her throat, she walked over to the front window. With a sigh of relief she watched Wilson step off the end of her driveway, open the front door of his car and get in.

Mike started the car but paused before he started driving. Why did he have the feeling that something about Jamie's answers sounded rehearsed?

13

While Mike Wilson focused on the four girls whose text messages were on Kerry's phone, detectives from the Prosecutor's Office met at the homes of Kerry's other friends who had been at the party. In most cases the mother or father or both sat in. Usually they sat on the couch on either side of their son or daughter, so tightly together that their arms were squeezing each other.

Detective Harsh, who began the questioning, started with a statement to put them at ease. "I want you to know right off the bat that this investigation is not about trying to charge or arrest anyone who was engaged in underage drinking that night. We know that a lot of people were. There were vodka and beer bottles all over the Dowling home and property. We don't know if anyone was using drugs that night. We do have to ask if you were drinking or using any drugs because it's possible that that could have affected your perceptions that night or your memory today. But again, we're not looking to get anyone in trouble for those reasons. What we do want to know is if there were any arguments or fights that night, particularly any that involved Kerry Dowling."

There had been thirty-one individuals at Kerry's party. Eight girls had witnessed Alan and Kerry having an argument. None of the girls admitted to having anything more than a couple of beers. They all adamantly denied that there were any drugs at the party.

One of the girls, Kate, who described herself as Kerry's best friend, cried as she spoke. "Alan got furious because Chris Kobel kept hanging around Kerry and talking about all the fun they were going to have at Boston College. It was clear that he wanted to go out with her. I hoped they would start going out. I thought Alan was being a jerk."

"Why did you think that?"

"Because he's so possessive of Kerry. In June, when he heard Chris had asked Kerry to go to the senior prom, he told Chris that Kerry was his girl and never to ask her out again. I told Kerry that Chris was a much nicer guy than Alan and she should smarten up and dump Alan.

"Then at the party Alan had been drinking a lot of beer. He picked a fight with Chris. Kerry stepped between them and started yelling at Alan. He took off and slammed the door behind him."

"How did Kerry react to that?"

"She looked upset for a minute but then she shrugged it off and said, 'Forget it.' "

"What time did Alan leave?"

"I'm not sure. It was ten-thirty, maybe quarter of eleven."

"Did Alan come back?"

"No."

"And what time did the party break up?"

"We all got out by eleven. That's when neighbors call the cops if there's any noise."

"Did anyone help Kerry clean up?"

"She said she'd do it herself. She wanted all the parked cars off the block by eleven o'clock. Kerry was very nervous about what she would do if a cop showed up when the party was still going."

"I have two last questions. Did you go out on the patio at any point in the evening?"

"Oh, sure I did."

"Did you notice a golf club out there?"

"Oh, yes. I did. The Dowlings are big golfers. They have a practice putting green on the side lawn. A couple of the guys were putting with it."

14

The unreality of what had happened to Kerry was a nightmare that dominated the few hours that Aline managed to doze on Sunday night. The events from the first moment she had found Kerry's body in the pool were a soundtrack running at fast-forward speed.

The cop doing CPR and then shaking his head.

The detective herding them into the house.

Trying to absorb the unspeakable.

Father Frank trying to make sense of the senseless.

Neighbors pouring in, offering to help in any way they can. Help with what?

Grandpa Dowling in the nursing home in Florida, who would be too sick to make the trip.

Mom's mother and father would be flying in tomorrow.

People bringing in food that they could only pick at.

Mom's constant sobbing.

Dad, white-faced, lips tight. His expression grief-stricken, trying to offer comfort to Mom and me.

The exhaustion of the flight home and the time change made it possible for me to fall asleep for an hour or so.

And then the kaleidoscope began.

At seven o'clock Aline sat up, threw aside the covers and dragged herself out of bed. The day, cloudy and promising rain, was in keeping with the way she felt.

She had tied back her long brown hair with a scrunchie, but it had slipped off during the night. She went over to the mirror on the dresser opposite the bed. It was as though Kerry was standing beside her, staring into it. Kerry looked like Mom with her golden blonde hair. Sparkling blue eyes. Perfect features.

Aline was her father's child, with hazel eyes, a thin face and deep brown hair. "Mud-colored," she told herself.

Her eyes were filled with grief, and she could see that she was very pale. Her pajamas were hanging loosely on her. She knew that Kerry would have taken one glance at her and said, "Look what the cat dragged in!" An involuntary smile came to her lips and disappeared.

She tiptoed down to the kitchen and made a pot of coffee. Ted Goldberg, a doctor and friend of her parents' from the golf club, had come over late yesterday afternoon and given her parents sleep aids. Aline hoped that the pills they had taken before going to bed last night had worked and were giving them a measure of peace.

She had taken on the task yesterday afternoon of phoning family members and close friends about the tragedy. Some were already aware after seeing news reports. It had been a comfort to read the stream of tributes that came pouring onto her sister's Facebook page. In the evening their next-door neighbor had brought in dinner. No one had been hungry, but they had all nibbled and felt better for it.

Her father had turned on the television at six-thirty. A picture of their house was on the screen. The lead story was about Kerry's murder. He had rushed to click it off.

Ordinarily Aline would have turned on the morning news the moment she entered the kitchen. But she didn't want to watch stories about Kerry. Not yet. Not ever.

She had left her cell phone in the dining room after making the calls. Coffee cup in hand, she went over to get it. She saw there was a voice message from a number she did not recognize. It had been left only an hour ago. It was from Mike Wilson, the detective who was handling Kerry's case. His image flashed into her mind. Handsome, a little over six feet tall, intense dark brown eyes, a slender athletic frame. A way of leaning forward, hands clasped as though to avoid missing any word that was said.

She tapped on the message. *Ms. Dowling, I know how rough everything is for you at this point, but I need your help. I hope I'm not calling too early. I understand that you are a guidance counselor at Saddle River High School. I think you could be a great help to me. Please call me as soon as you get this message.*

Without trying to analyze the reason she could be of help to him, Aline returned the call. When he heard her voice, Mike Wilson went straight to the point. "Based on what I have learned so far, there were about thirty individuals at the party, and I have most of the names. I believe most of them were Kerry's year, which means they will be leaving imminently for college. I want to find out which colleges they are going to and when they will be leaving. For obvious reasons, I want to talk first to those leaving earliest. Can you help me with this?"

"I'm glad you called. I had totally forgotten I'm supposed to be at the high school at one o'clock today for an orientation meeting. I may be able to help you. Today's training would include instruction on how to use the computer system."

"Are you planning to go?"

"Frankly, I could use a little distraction. You asked about when colleges start. Here's a quick rule of thumb. Southern schools in mid-August. They're back already. Catholic schools around Labor Day. The Ivies in mid-September. Most of the others around now, the last week in August."

"I really appreciate this. I'm sorry to ask you to go in only a day after —"

She cut him off. "I'm glad to have something helpful to do. Text me the names and I'll get you the schools."

"That would be great, Ms. Dowling."

"Please call me Aline."

"Okay, Aline. And one last request, would you also have the dates of birth in your records? I have to know which ones are adults and which are minors."

"I can get those too. You'll have them by late afternoon."

Aline felt strange as she maneuvered her car into a space reserved for FACULTY at the high school. The parking lot was nearly empty.

She knocked on the half-open door to the principal's office. Pat Tarleton quickly rose from her desk, walked over and embraced her. "I'm so sorry, honey. How are you and your parents doing?"

"We're all in shock trying to absorb what happened. I thought it would be good to force my mind to focus on something else, so I wanted to keep our appointment."

Pat guided Aline over to a chair next to hers where they could both see the large screen on her desktop computer. She handed her a piece of paper with some scribbling on it. "This is your password to access our computer system. Let me show you how it works."

Aline quickly absorbed Pat's instructions. Fortunately, the system was very similar to the one she had used at the International School. When they were finished, Pat handed her a list she had printed out. "These are all the teachers and personnel at the school and their contact information."

As Aline skimmed the list, she was pleasantly surprised to see that many of the teachers she'd had were still at the school. "It feels like old home week," she told Pat as she attempted a smile.

15

Marge didn't know what to do. Had that detective been able to see that Jamie wasn't telling the truth? The way Jamie kept looking at her for approval might be misinterpreted. That Detective Wilson seemed very smart.

As always when she was upset, Marge reached for her rosary beads. Before she began to recite the first Sorrowful Mystery, the Agony in the Garden, she began to think of Jack. His image was never far from her heart and mind. She had met him at an amusement park in Rye. He was a senior at All Hallows High School and she was a junior at St. Jean's. She lived in the Bronx and took the subway to school on East 75th Street in Manhattan. He lived on West 200th Street and would be going to Fordham in September. She told him that she was planning to go to Marymount in two years.

We didn't leave each other's side even for a minute until his group got back on the boat and the nuns called us to our bus.

I thought Jack was the handsomest man I had ever laid eyes on, tall and with that blonde hair and blue eyes. Jamie is the image of him. He told me the Chapman name was on very old tombstones at Cape Cod, where his ancestors were buried. They weren't on the *Mayflower,* but they arrived not much after, Jack told me. He was so proud of that, she thought tenderly.

My Irish father was from a farm family in Roscommon. He was younger than his brother, which meant his brother would inherit the farm. So when he was twenty, he said goodbye to his parents, sisters and brothers and sailed to New York. He met my mother there, and they got married when she was nineteen and he was twenty-two.

Like us when we got married, Marge thought. I was twenty and left college after my sophomore year. Jack was twenty-four. He had left college after his freshman year, deciding instead to get his electrician's license. He liked working in construction.

Oh, Jack, I wish you were here now. We had given up hope of having a baby, and then when I was forty-five I became pregnant. After all those years of hoping and then accepting that God didn't want to send us children, it was a miracle. We were so happy, she thought. Then we almost lost Jamie when he was born. He was deprived of oxygen, but he was ours.

Jack had the heart attack and died when Jamie was fifteen. The poor little guy kept looking all over for him and crying, "Daddy!"

Jack, I'm looking for you to help me now, Marge prayed. Maybe Jamie thought he was playing a game with Kerry, poor girl. But she had a blow on her head. He'd never do that. I'm sure of it.

But the cops could twist his story if they knew he had been in the pool with her. Can you imagine him going to prison? He'd be so frightened, and men take advantage of a boy like him.

It can't happen. It just can't happen.

Marge looked down at the rosary she was holding. As she began her prayer, Jamie came down from his room, where he had been watching television.

"I didn't tell anyone about going swimming with Kerry," he said. "Wasn't that good?"

16

Aline loved her grandparents. Both in their late seventies, they had moved to Arizona because of her grandmother's chronic arthritis. She had been sure that their arrival would combine both comfort and strained nerves.

The minute they were in the door, her grandmother, shoulders slouching, her arthritic fingers clutching a cane, wailed, "It should have been me. Why this beautiful child? Why? Why?"

Aline's first thought was, Because you never go into pools! Her grandfather, strong and healthy for his age, said, "I understand she was having a party when you people were away. That's what happens when kids are left unsupervised."

It was more of an accusation than a consolation. "That's what I've been telling Steve," Fran chimed in.

Aline exchanged a glance with her father.

She knew her grandparents had always felt her mother should have married the man she was briefly engaged to thirty years ago. He had gone on to work in Silicon Valley and was now a tech billionaire. Her father, a partner in an accounting firm, made a very good income, but it did not include a private plane, a yacht, a mansion in Connecticut or a villa in Florence.

Normally her father let their criticism roll off his back. Aline was worried about how he would react this time. A roll of his eyes was their unspoken message: "Don't worry; they'll be gone in three or four days."

On Wednesday Aline suggested to her father that she go with him to make arrangements for a wake on Thursday and a funeral on Friday morning. She was afraid her mother would have a total breakdown if she had to choose a casket. But it was her mother who decided that Kerry would be buried in the gown she had worn to her senior prom. It was a beautiful pale blue, full-length organdy, and Kerry had looked lovely in it.

At one o'clock on Thursday afternoon, dressed in newly purchased black clothes, the family gathered solemnly in the funeral home. When Fran saw Kerry's body in the casket, she fainted.

"Why, why?" Aline's grandmother wailed, as Steve caught his wife before she collapsed. But Fran did manage to find enough inner strength to be on the receiving line when visitors started arriving.

As news cameras clicked from their locations across the street, the neighbors, teachers and students from the high school, and friends from long ago, arrived. By three o'clock the line looped around the block.

Aline found herself watching to see if Alan Crowley would appear. But there was no sign of him. She didn't know whether to be relieved or angry. Remembering the way her mother felt about him, she knew it was better that he had not shown his face.

Some of Kerry's former lacrosse team members arrived with the coach, Scott Kimball. He was an attractive man with a disciplined body and dark brown hair. Wearing high heels, Aline was eye-level with him.

He had tears in his eyes as he took Aline's hand on the receiving line.

"I know how you feel," he said. "My kid brother was killed by a hit-and-run driver when he was fifteen. There isn't a day goes by that I don't think of him."

It was impossible to imagine daily life without Kerry.

The haunting question of who had murdered her was on everyone's mind. Aline heard her mother tell people she was absolutely convinced it was Alan Crowley. "I was trying to keep her away from him," Fran murmured. "With all the boys who were interested in Kerry, why she chose that one, I don't know. He was always so jealous of her. He had a bad temper. Now look what he's done to her."

There was a hint of early September in the air on the morning of the funeral. Even though the sun was shining brightly, the breeze was cool. Following Kerry's casket up the aisle in the processional renewed Aline's sense of unreality and detachment. Kerry and I should be at the pool together going over what stuff she should take to college, she thought, not here. Not here.

Father Frank's homily was comforting. As he said, "We do not understand why these tragedies occur. It is only faith that gives us the comfort we need." Father Frank told again the story of looking at life from the wrong side of the beautiful Persian rug. To Aline it had even more meaning than when he was with them the day she found Kerry in the pool.

The question of whether Alan would dare to show up was constantly on her mind. She watched as people approached the Communion rail, but did not see him or his parents. That was a relief. The sight of him would have driven Mom crazy, she thought. But as Aline and her parents followed the casket out of the church, she did catch a glimpse of Alan. He was kneeling in the last pew in the far corner, his head buried in his hands.

17

Because of her stepfather's job transfer, sophomore Valerie Long and her family had moved from Chicago to Saddle River. The transition was made even harder because they had moved over Christmas and she had started at the high school in January.

Tall for her age and looking younger than her sixteen years, she had green eyes, jet-black hair and pale skin. The promise of future beauty was in her face. Valerie was an only child, and her widowed mother had remarried when she was five. Her stepfather was twenty years older than her mother. They rarely saw his two grown children, who lived in California. Valerie was sure he considered her excess baggage. Her timid and retiring nature had resulted in extreme shyness.

Last winter at school Valerie had found herself outside already formed cliques and friendships. This made the adjustment even harder. It was in the spring that things began to change for her.

Fast and well coordinated, she had excelled at lacrosse freshman year at her previous school. She was hoping that if she made the team at Saddle River, that would create easy opportunities to make new friendships. As usual things did not work out the way she expected.

Coach Scott Kimball immediately recognized her talent and put her on the varsity squad. The varsity was all seniors except for two juniors and her. She would have preferred to play on the junior varsity with the sophomores and freshmen, but she didn't want to disappoint the coach or her teammates.

It was Kerry, the team captain, who first admired Valerie's skill on the field and also recognized how shy she was. Kerry went out of her way to chat with Valerie and tell her how good she was. She became, in essence, her big sister and the closest thing Valerie had to a confidante.

Kerry's sudden death was a stunning blow to Valerie. She could not bring herself to go to either the wake or the funeral, but stood alone across the street watching the casket leaving the church and being lifted onto the hearse. When she walked away, she was still unable to feel the release of tears.

18

Marge's close friend was the Crowleys' housekeeper, Brenda. Brenda and her husband Curt, a retired plumber, lived in Westwood, New Jersey, a few miles from Saddle River. Curt Niemeier had often worked on construction projects with Jack Chapman. Like Jack and Marge, the Niemeiers had lived in a small Saddle River ranch house before the price of real estate had gone up dramatically. They had sold and bought a house in nearby Westwood and a small place at the Jersey Shore.

While Curt was enjoying retirement, Brenda found herself restless. In the early years of their marriage she had been a housekeeper to bring in extra money. She realized she had enjoyed the work and was good at it. "Some people go to a gym. I get my exercise by cleaning." She decided to look for that kind of work to fill her days. The result was she worked three days a week as a combination housekeeper and cook.

She and Marge had remained close over the years, and when she confided gossip to Marge, Brenda knew it would not go any further. A medium-sized woman with short gray hair and narrow shoulders, she liked her job at the Crowleys', but did not like them. She considered June Crowley stuck-up and cheap, and her husband full of himself and a total bore. The one person in the family she cared about was Alan. The poor kid got stuck with those two. In their eyes, he can't do anything right. When he gets an A in school, it should have been an A+.

I know he's got a temper, Brenda often thought to herself, but I swear those two drive him to it.

Their constant hope was that in September Alan would be enrolled in an Ivy League college so they could brag to their friends.

They're always after him, Brenda confided to Marge. "If I were in his boots, I'd have applied to the University of Hawaii just to get away from them.

"Of course, I wasn't there over the weekend when that poor girl was killed. But I gather that when the Crowleys found out that a cop had come over and talked to

Alan, they hit the ceiling. And now all I hear around town is that everyone thinks that Alan did it.

"The way the Crowleys are carrying on, I swear I wonder if they don't think so themselves."

19

The business of picking up the pieces after Kerry's death began to fall into place. Aline helped her mother with the personal notes to the people who had sent floral tributes to the wake.

By unspoken understanding they had closed the door to Kerry's room. The bed, still freshly made, was covered by the blue-and-white coverlet Kerry had chosen when she was sixteen.

Her clothes were in the closet. The woolly Lassie dog that she had carried under her arm when she was a toddler was perched on a bench in front of the window.

Originally the plan was to place Lassie in the casket with her, but at the last minute Fran had told Steve and Aline that she wanted to keep it.

Fran had been adamant that they find a contractor to "demo" the pool, to remove any trace that it had ever existed. Steve had persuaded her to compromise. They would close the pool for the season. They would decide next spring if they should get rid of it.

In these ten days before school opened Aline had tried to sort out her own thinking. Kerry and I were different siblings hatched in the same nest, she thought. Kerry was so beautiful from the moment she opened her eyes.

Aline was ten years old then, too skinny, with teeth that obviously would need to be straightened, and mousy brown hair that hung limp on her shoulders.

But I adored her. There wasn't ever sibling rivalry. It was just that we were two different people. I used to beg mom to be the one who pushed her in the baby carriage.

But then there were other differences. From day one I was a voracious reader. I threw myself into books. I wanted to be Jane Eyre, or Catherine running on the moors with Heathcliff. I wanted to show how smart I was. From the first grade I wanted to be first in the class and I made it.

The only sport I got into was tennis, and I loved it because it was so competitive. "Forty-love" was music to my ears.

Columbia was my first choice for college, and I got in. Then a master's degree in psychology.

And then becoming engaged to Rick. He was a graduate student when we met, and then that was it for both of us. His height made me feel small, so protected.

He was relatively local, from Hastings-on-Hudson, only forty minutes from Saddle River. Rick used to say his ambition was to get his doctorate and then teach in college, Aline mused. I told him I wanted to teach in high school and/or become a guidance counselor. I had just completed my master's and he his doctorate when we set the date for our wedding.

Four years ago. We had made all the arrangements for the big day. Mom and I picked out my gown. I was going to wear her veil, Aline remembered. We had dinner here that night and then Rick drove home.

The call from his father had come three hours later. Rick had a head-on collision with a drunk driver and died in the hospital. The drunk driver didn't have a scratch.

How did I pick up the pieces? Aline asked herself. I knew I had to get away. That was why I took the job at the International School in London.

Three years ago. Only coming home for Thanksgiving and Christmas. Three years of waiting for the pain to ease, and then finally beginning to wake up in the morning without Rick being the first thought on my mind.

Three years of casual dates since then, but never any interest in letting them progress.

And this last year the need had come to be home, to be in daily contact with her parents and all the friends she had left behind.

Instead she had returned to find the little sister she loved a murder victim. There *is* something I can do, she thought, and that is to be here for them. She had intended to get her own apartment in Manhattan, but that could wait.

Who had taken Kerry's life? Who could have done that to someone who had so much promise, who had her whole life to live?

It's not going to happen again, Aline vowed. Whoever took Kerry's life is going to pay the price for it. I like Mike Wilson. I think he's smart and capable. But how can I help him?

There was one possible way. Most of the kids who were at the party would be back in school. If any of them knew more than they were telling Mike and the other cops, maybe they'd be more loose-lipped as time passed.

The police may be zeroing in on Alan Crowley, Aline thought. But from what I gather, the evidence against him is strong but not overwhelming.

Since graduating from high school, Aline had remained in close touch with the principal, Pat Tarleton. A month earlier Pat had emailed her about an opening in the Guidance Department. Would she be interested?

It was the job she wanted, and the timing was right. With Kerry having graduated, she would be spared the awkwardness of having her big sister work at the same school.

20

Marge was living in a state of suspended animation. Instinctively she had felt that when Detective Wilson stopped in the day Kerry's body was found, he had observed Jamie looking for her approval. Although she believed he had not told anyone about going into Kerry's pool, it was always possible he would blurt it out to someone. It didn't help that sometimes out of the blue he would refer back to it with her.

"Mom, I didn't tell anybody about going swimming with Kerry."

Her reassurances were quick and hushed. "That's our secret, dear. We don't talk about secrets."

Every day, when she left him at the Acme market, she held her breath until she picked him up. Without realizing why, she found herself driving him both ways, instead of letting him walk.

As soon as he got home, she would ask

him who he had talked to at work and what they had spoken about. Sometimes he would finish his answer with a triumphant smile. "And I didn't tell anybody I went swimming with Kerry." Marge was conflicted. She wanted to keep track of anyone he was speaking to. On the other hand, were these conversations making him think even more about what happened the night Kerry died?

It made things worse when he suddenly began to talk about "the Big Guy" in the woods. Jack's affectionate nickname for Jamie was "the Big Guy." Trying to sound casual, she asked him, "What about the Big Guy, Jamie?"

"He hit Kerry and pushed her in the pool," he said matter-of-factly.

Marge forced herself to ask, "Jamie, who is the Big Guy?"

"Daddy called me the Big Guy. Remember, Mom?"

Her throat went dry. Marge whispered, "I remember, Jamie. I remember."

Marge knew that she could not bear the burden alone. Her consuming worry was that the police might try to blame Jamie, especially since he had told them about swimming with Kerry, but she knew it wasn't right to hide the truth from them.

The previous evening Jamie had told her a big guy had come around from the bushes after the first guy left, and he had hit Kerry on the head and pushed her in the pool.

But if Jamie told that to the police, they would compare him to Alan Crowley. Alan was medium height and on the thin side. Jamie was six feet, one inch, and not fat but broad. Sometime he calls himself "Big Guy," Marge thought. If he says this to the police, they might think that "the Big Guy" Jamie was describing was actually Jamie himself. If they believe that, they might arrest him.

He'd be so frightened. He's so easily manipulated. He always wants to please. He'll happily say anything they want to hear.

Marge felt again the familiar tightness in her chest. Her doctor had warned her to take a nitroglycerin tablet whenever that happened. By the end of the day she had taken three tablets.

Dear God, don't let anything happen to me, she begged. He needs me now more than ever.

21

Mike's next stops were the homes of the four girls who had texted Kerry after the party. Each set of their parents had agreed to allow their daughter to talk.

He rang the bell of Betsy Finley and met her and her parents. He was invited to come into the living room. Betsy sat on a couch, wedged between her parents. Wilson settled into a chair opposite the couch.

He began by saying, as Detective Harsh had said during his interviews, that he had no intention of arresting anyone solely for drinking or having any drugs, but that it was very important that Betsy be honest with him. He emphasized that his only interest was in finding out what had happened to Kerry.

He tried to make his questions sound casual. After Betsy sheepishly admitted that she had one or two vodkas, they established what time Betsy got to the party and what time she left. Wilson asked, "Were there any fights or disagreements at the party?"

Of course, Betsy immediately told him that Alan and Kerry had an argument because Kerry and Chris Kobel were flirting with each other. And after the quarrel, Alan left before anyone else. She told Mike that everyone else left in a group because Kerry wanted them all out by eleven o'clock.

The interview turned out to be simply a verification of what Mike knew from the texts and his interview of Alan.

His final question was "Do you know who brought in the beer and vodka?" It drew a shake of Betsy's head.

"It was already there when I arrived, and I was the first one to get to the party."

Similar answers came from the next two girls who had texted Kerry. The one who'd sent the "Dump Alan" text heatedly exclaimed that Alan wasn't just upset or annoyed; he was ballistic.

It was the last girl who had texted Kerry after the party who proved the most valuable to Mike. When he asked her who brought the liquor to the party, her answer was "Kerry told me that the guy who fixed the flat tire on her car had told her that anytime she had a party, he could get her

101

whatever alcohol she wanted."

Mike did not show any change of expression. "Do you know the name of the guy who fixed the flat?"

"I don't."

"Did Kerry describe him or say where she met him?"

"I think she got the flat on Route 17 in Mahwah, and he pulled over to help."

"Did she say where she met him to get the alcohol for the party?"

"No, but she did tell me that when she met him to pick it up, he put it in her trunk. Then when she closed the trunk, he asked her if he could come to the party. She told him it was just for her high school friends. There wouldn't be anybody his age there. Kerry said this guy was about twenty-five. Then he said, 'Well, maybe we can get together after your friends go home.' Of course, she said no. Then he grabbed her and started kissing her."

"Did she ever describe this guy to you?"

"No. Right after she told him to get lost, she told me she got in her car and drove off."

"So she didn't say where she met him to pick up the alcohol?"

"I don't think she did. I can't remember."

He looked at her parents. "I'm very grateful to have had this opportunity to talk with your daughter."

He said goodbye and left to go back to his car. As he drove away, he could only think about the fact that there might just be yet another potential suspect in Kerry Dowling's murder.

22

The sun was streaming through the windows of the rectory. Marge sat opposite Father Frank in his office. Instead of sitting behind his desk, he had pulled up a chair closer to her.

"Marge, I'm happy you've come to see me. I could tell from your voice on the phone that you are very upset. What's wrong?"

"Jamie, he's in trouble."

There was a pause. And then Marge, her voice trembling began, "Father, from his window Jamie was watching the party at Kerry Dowling's house. When she fell or was pushed into the pool, he thought she went swimming and went over to swim with her."

"Did he tell you that?"

"Not at first. The next morning I noticed that his slacks were wet and so were his socks and sneakers. When I asked him about it, he told me he had seen someone come up behind Kerry, hit her and push her in the pool. Still thinking he could go swimming with her, he walked down the steps to the pool."

Marge took a deep breath.

"I didn't know what to do, Father. I watched that awful scene of Steve Dowling and Aline finding Kerry in the pool. I was afraid. Afraid for Jamie. His sneakers and pants had stains on them. Maybe it was wrong, but I washed them. I had to protect Jamie. I made Jamie promise not to talk to anybody about what happened that night."

"Marge, what Jamie saw could be very helpful to the police."

"Yes, but it could also get Jamie in a lot of trouble if they think he did it." Marge drew a deep breath. "Father, that's not all. Remember how Jack always called Jamie 'Big Guy'?"

"Of course I remember."

"And now Jamie has been talking to me about 'the Big Guy' who pushed Kerry into the pool. Alan Crowley is average height and has a thin build. Jamie sometimes talks about himself as 'the Big Guy.' He can get mixed up if he's upset. I'm so afraid that if he ever tells that to the police . . ." Marge's voice trailed off.

"Marge, is there any chance Jamie might have hurt Kerry?"

"Jamie was disappointed and maybe even angry that he wasn't invited to the party, but I can't see him ever hurting her."

"But when Jamie said a 'Big Guy' pushed Kerry in the pool. Do *you* think he may have been talking about himself?"

Marge sighed. "I don't know what to think. He loved her. I can't believe he would hurt her. A detective came by and spoke to us. I don't think he suspects Jamie, but I just don't know."

"Marge, I don't want to give you quick advice that might turn out to be wrong. Let me think about what we've discussed."

"Thank you so much, Father. And please pray for me. And for Jamie."

"I will, Marge. I promise."

23

Excited by the start of a new school year, students poured back into the hallways. As they passed Aline, many of them stopped to tell her how sorry they were about Kerry. Aline tried to keep her eyes from welling up as one after the other they told her they couldn't believe what had happened to her sister. "Neither can I" was her answer.

The day passed by in a blur. After the school buses had come and gone and the teachers began to go home, Aline sat in her office. She tried to familiarize herself with the names of this year's seniors. She knew that one of her jobs would be to help them finalize which colleges they would apply to.

She was troubled by the fact that the first thing she had done on the computer was to look up the information requested by Mike Wilson. She worried that if they found out what she had given to the detective, her first day at Saddle River High School could be her last. She hoped not.

There was a tap on her door. Pat Tarleton opened it and came in. "So Aline, how did the first day go?"

"As well as can be expected," Aline said wryly. "That said, it feels good to be here. And I'm looking forward to getting to know the students and my fellow faculty."

"Speaking of that, I noticed that you and Scott Kimball were chatting in the teachers' lounge together. He's been a great addition to the faculty this past year. His math classes have been very popular with the students. And he's been a godsend for the girls lacrosse program."

"He had some of the players at the wake with him," Aline said, her tone noncommittal.

"And I remember Kerry talking about what a great coach he was. Okay, I just wanted to pop by. See you in the A.M."

The door had barely closed behind Pat when Aline's cell phone rang. It was Mike Wilson.

"Aline, when Kerry was in touch with you, whether by phone, text or email, did she ever mention somebody stopping to help her with a flat?"

In her mind Aline raced through her recent emails from Kerry. "No, I don't recall that. I assume there's a reason you're asking."

"I'm just trying to be thorough. One of Kerry's friends told me that someone who helped her change a flat got a little aggressive with her after she refused to invite him to the party. It's probably nothing. But I want to find out that person's name."

"Do you think he may have been the one who . . . ?"

"Aline, we follow up on anything that might turn out to be relevant. That's why I need to ask your folks about the flat tire."

"Of course."

"How are they doing?"

"I know going back to work is helping my father. My mother is pretty bad."

"Will they be home this evening? Kerry might have talked to them about the flat and who helped her. Do you know what time might be convenient for them?"

"Dad is usually home by six-thirty. We never eat before seven-thirty. I would say about six-forty-five."

"Fine. I'll see you then as well."

Aline pushed the button to power down her computer. She was about to get out of her chair when there was another knock on the door. Scott Kimball came into her office.

The lacrosse coach was also a mathematics instructor, teaching courses in algebra, geometry and calculus. It was the beginning of his second year at this school. He had been hired a year earlier to replace a retiring teacher, and the athletic director had been delighted to find in Kimball someone who had played lacrosse and was willing to coach it. He was quickly made head coach of the girls' varsity squad.

"Just a social visit," he said. "How is it going?"

"My grandparents have gone back to Arizona. I'll miss them, but in a way it's easier. My dad went back to work. My mother is having a really hard time. Of course, we all are. But she's determined to keep as busy as possible."

"Aline, I know the timing may not be right, it might be premature, but I'm going to plow forward anyway. I would very much enjoy taking you to dinner. I've been dying to try a new French restaurant that opened right on the Hudson in Nyack. I'm told the food and the view are both great."

Aline hesitated. Undoubtedly Scott was an attractive man. But she wasn't sure if it was wise to *socialize* — oh come on, call it what it really is — *date* a fellow staffer. "I'm not ready yet, but can we talk about it in a couple weeks?"

"Absolutely. As you know, I'll be around."
With a wave he left her office.

Aline thought of Kerry's reaction to Kimball at the end of last season. He's a great coach and a really nice guy. He was so much better than the former coach, Don Brown, who had no idea what he was doing. Score one for you, Kerry, Aline thought. It seems like you would have approved of my joining Scott Kimball for dinner at the restaurant with the great view.

She locked her door behind her and headed out to the parking lot.

24

True to his word, Mike Wilson rang the doorbell at precisely 6:45. Aline had told her parents that he wanted to stop in. Her mother's reaction was instant. "He's going to tell us that they've arrested Alan Crowley."

"No, it's not about that at all. It's just a question he has for you."

Steve asked, "About Kerry?"

"Yes, it's about a flat tire Kerry had."

"Kerry never had a flat tire," Steve said firmly.

"Well, tell Detective Wilson that."

When Mike arrived, Aline wanted to avoid having the meeting in the family room. That was where the three of them had been sitting when Mike told them that Kerry's death was not an accident. Instead she suggested that they go into the living room.

When they were seated, Mike explained the reason for the meeting, reporting what he had told Aline. Steve said firmly, "Kerry said nothing about getting a flat. But I had told her that the rear tire on her car was looking threadbare. And I wanted her to go to the dealer and have it changed right away. If she had a flat before she took care of it, she would not have wanted to tell us about it."

"Did she ever get a new tire?" Mike asked.

"She showed me she got the new one about ten days ago."

"Doesn't that narrow the time when she met whoever changed the flat and sold her the beer for the party?" Aline asked.

"And then tried to force himself on her," Steve said bitterly.

"Yes, assuming she got the replacement tire right after getting the flat." Mike got up. "This could be very helpful in following up on whoever that guy is."

"The only one you should be concentrating on is Alan Crowley," Fran said firmly as her eyes filled with tears.

Aline walked Mike to the door. "I wonder if Mom is right about Alan Crowley?" she asked.

"We try to avoid fixating on one obvious suspect. We're determined to pursue any relevant leads." He repeated the question Pat Tarleton had asked. "How did your first day go?"

"A little overwhelming, of course. But I have a question. Does anyone else know I gave you the information about the birth dates and where they're going to college?"

"No one knows where I got that information."

"Good. If it's okay, I'd like to keep it that way."

"Absolutely. Good night."

Aline watched his retreating figure and waited until he stepped into the car and drove away.

Valerie endured the first day of school as though she was walking in her sleep. Every step of the way it felt like Kerry was there. Kerry on the lacrosse field. Kerry walking with her arm around her as they headed to the locker room.

Inside, Valerie so much wanted to be able to cry. But somehow the tears were all stuck in her throat.

As she was changing classes, she saw Kerry's sister, the new guidance counselor, in the corridor. She was wearing a dark blue jacket and slacks. As she passed her, Valerie thought she was so pretty. She was taller than Kerry and her hair was dark brown, but they still looked a lot alike.

I'm sorry, Kerry, Valerie thought. I'm so sorry.

25

As they had planned, Alan Crowley's parents met the well-known defense lawyer Lester Parker. A reluctant Alan accompanied them.

"Alan, let us go over what happened at the party," Parker began. "Kerry Dowling was your girlfriend, wasn't she?"

"Yes, she was."

"How long were the two of you, um, in a relationship?"

"A year."

"Is it true you two had a lot of arguments?"

"Afterwards we joked about them. Kerry was a flirt and liked to see me get mad. But we always made up."

"What about the night of the party? Did you have a quarrel?"

"Kerry had had a couple vodkas. She never could handle any liquor well, even a glass or two of wine. So when Chris Kobel started flirting with her, she kept flirting back with him."

"Had you been drinking?"

"Yes, I just had a couple of beers."

"A couple?"

"Maybe three or four. I'm not really sure."

Alan was very aware that his parents were now glaring at him.

"I understand you left the party before it was over. Where did you go?"

"I knew some of my friends would be at a local pizza restaurant, Nellie's in Waldwick. I met them there."

"Did you stay with them until you went home?"

"No."

"Did you go directly to Kerry's house from the restaurant?"

"Yes."

"Where was she when you got there?"

"She was out on the patio in back of the house, cleaning up."

"What did she say when she saw you?"

She didn't say anything. I said, 'Kerry, I'm sorry. I just want to help you clean up.' "

"How did she respond to that?"

" 'I'm tired. I'm getting up early in the morning. I want to go to bed now.' "

"Did you leave then?"

"I could tell that she meant it. She was

yawning. So I said, 'I'll see you tomorrow.' "

"What happened next?"

"She said, 'Okay, let's talk tomorrow.' "

"And what did you do then?"

"I gave her a hug and a kiss and went home."

"What time did you get home?"

June jumped in. "We were in the bedroom. I looked at the clock. It was exactly eleven-fifty-one."

A look of annoyance came over Parker's face. "Alan, do you agree? Was it around eleven-fifty-one?"

"No, I think it was a little later."

"It was exactly eleven-fifty-one," June interjected. "As I told you, I was looking at the clock when Alan came in."

There was a pause, and then Lester Parker turned to the Crowleys. "I wonder if you would mind waiting outside. The best way I can help Alan is if I hear the facts directly from him."

When the door closed behind them, Parker said, "Alan, we have attorney-client privilege. Nothing you tell me will be shared with anyone. In any way shape or form, did you either hit Kerry or push her in the pool?"

"Absolutely not." Alan's expression and body language were fiercely defensive.

"How would you feel if everyone in town thought you were a murderer?" he burst out. "How would you feel if your parents were so sure you were going to get arrested that they hired a hotshot lawyer to defend you? How would you feel if your girlfriend, who you really loved, got murdered?"

Alan's lips quivered. Lester Parker studied Alan. He had heard many defendants plead their innocence and could often detect who was lying and who was telling the truth. He was still reserving judgment on Alan Crowley as he prepared to offer a defense for him.

"When did you learn that Kerry was dead?"

"About noon on Sunday. I was outside mowing the lawn and my cell phone was in the house. When I went in to get a bottle of water, I could see there were a lot of messages and texts. I read one of the texts and found out what happened. As I was reading the message, a detective came to the house and asked me to go down to Hackensack with him."

"Did you tell him exactly what you're telling me?"

"Yes, I did."

"Alan, it must have been very scary for you to go down to the Prosecutors Office and get videotaped. Did you say anything in that interview that was not true?"

Alan hesitated.

"It's okay, Alan," Parker said. "You can tell me."

"I told the detective I stayed at the restaurant with my friends the whole time and then I went straight home from there. I didn't tell him I went to see Kerry on the way home."

"Okay. Sunday morning you wake up. I understand your parents left early to play golf. You mowed the lawn until the detective came and you went with him to Hackensack. Did you go anywhere or talk to anyone after you got back from Hackensack and before your parents got home?"

Alan was silent for a moment. Parker put down his pen and said gently, "Alan, the only way I can effectively help you is if you are honest with me."

"When I got back from Hackensack, I was freaking out. I needed somebody to back up my story that I went straight home from Nellie's."

"So what did you do?"

"I called one of the guys I was with. The two other guys were at his house. I asked them to back me up that I stayed at Nellie's as late as they did."

"Do you know if they've spoken to the

police?"

"Yes, they have."

"Okay."

Alan gave Parker the names of his three friends and their contact information.

Alan said, "Look, I know I panicked, and I screwed up. And I know that by lying, I've made it worse. What can I do to start making things right?"

Parker looked directly at his client. "There are two things you can do. From now on, aside from your parents and me, talk to no one about the case. If anyone contacts you, refer him to me."

Alan nodded.

"The other thing you can do is when you go home, tell your parents what you just told me. They're going to find out anyway, so let's get that difficult discussion behind us right away."

26

In the morning at breakfast Steve announced that he was coming home early and he and Fran were going to the movies. Fran had not yet come down from their room. Over a quick second cup of coffee he said to Aline, "I think I need to get your mother out of the house. I told her that last night after Detective Wilson left, and she agreed. She's so fixated on the idea that Alan Crowley murdered Kerry that she's telling that to everybody she speaks to. I told her that until there is real proof, we have to keep an open mind. But even after all that Detective Wilson told us about the man who sold Kerry the beer, she is still fixated on Alan's guilt."

Steve carried his empty coffee mug over and placed it in the sink. "One night every week a theater in Norwood is running the old classics. Greer Garson is still one of your mother's favorite actors. She'll enjoy seeing

Random Harvest on the big screen. It starts at five o'clock, and then I'll take her out to dinner. Do you want to join us for the movie, dinner or both?"

"Thanks, Dad, but I'll pass. I want to catch up on some stuff at school. I'll pick up something for dinner on the way home."

The next day at school was a little easier than the one before. Aline had always been good at remembering names and faces. After she passed one of the students in the hallway, she remembered that she had seen her before and where it was. This was the girl who had been standing across the street from the church when the Mass for Kerry was over. I wonder why she didn't come in, Aline asked herself.

She was in her office until six. She had left her door partially open and Scott Kimball looked in. "Obviously working late again," he said.

"A little," Aline replied.

"Is there any chance that when you're ready to wrap up, you'll have dinner with me? I know I asked you only yesterday, but the question just popped into my head. You know, it might be a nice change."

"Are you tempting me with the French restaurant you were talking about?"

"Absolutely."

Then my answer is *"Oui."*

They laughed together.

Aline declined Scott's offer to ride with him and instead took her own car to La Petite restaurant. Scott had told her he lived in Fort Lee. Driving her back to pick up her car at school would take him way out of his way.

On the way over, she started to have second thoughts. She berated herself for agreeing to go to dinner with him. She went over in her head why it was foolish to alter the business relationship of two faculty members who worked in the same school. Just this once, she told herself, absolutely just this once.

She began to relax at the restaurant. La Petite turned out to be every bit as good as Scott had promised. In the three years she had taught at the International School in London, it had been easy to take the train through the Chunnel to Paris. It was a trip she had made every few months while she lived in England. She would stay at a small hotel on the Left Bank that overlooked Notre Dame Cathedral. She made regular visits to the Louvre and other museums, as well as boat trips on the Seine.

Along the way she had developed a passion for French food. At the same time she had perfected her natural gift for languages. Her goal was to become fluent in French and to speak it without an American accent. When their waiter introduced himself with a French accent, she saw an opportunity to practice.

Scott then surprised her by following her lead. His command of French was very good, but his American accent was clearly discernible.

After listening to the specials, they gave their orders. As they sipped the Bordeaux Scott had chosen, he said, "I took a semester in France when I was in college. It was a program where I took courses in French and lived with a French family."

"Total immersion?" Aline asked.

"That was the idea," Scott chuckled. "But when I was with the other students, it was really easy to slip back to speaking English."

"I wish I had had an opportunity like that," Aline said.

"Whatever you did, your French is better than mine."

"There's a reason for that." She told him about her frequent trips to Paris.

They compared notes on different places they had visited in and around Paris. The conversation shifted to the high school, and

Scott shared his impressions of his fellow teachers and the administration. It was only over coffee that he brought up Kerry's name.

"Aline, I've had a wonderful time tonight. Part of me wants to tell you about how great a young woman Kerry was, but I'm reluctant to introduce a topic that might upset you."

"No, it's okay. I saw Kerry through the eyes of a big sister. If I had it to do over again, I would not have been away as much as I was the last three years. What was it like to be her coach?"

"She was really special. She wasn't the best player on the team, but she was very good, and she had a natural ability to lead. The best compliment you can give a player is that she made her teammates better when she was on the field."

When the evening ended and she was driving home, Aline realized that she had enjoyed the dinner very much. Scott was a very nice guy, and he was good company.

27

The results of the autopsy revealed that Kerry had been killed instantly by a massive blow to the back of her skull. There was almost no water in her lungs, indicating she had not been breathing after being struck. The alcohol level in her blood was .06, the equivalent of a person her size consuming two to three drinks. There was no evidence of sexual assault.

The State Lab's analysis of the golf club verified that it was the weapon that had been used on Kerry. The strands of hair on the head of the putter were matched with samples of her hair. The specks of blood lifted from the club contained Kerry's DNA.

Fingerprints on the rubber grip would be virtually impossible to collect, but there were five identifiable prints on the shaft that potentially could be matched.

Mike began the process of identifying the

prints by going first to Steve and Fran Dowling. It was as he had expected, a difficult meeting. Once again he swung by at about 6:45 P.M., when Steve would be home. When he explained his reason for being there, it caused Fran to cry out in near hysteria, "Are you telling me that our golf club was used to kill my little girl?"

"Fran, Detective Wilson is telling us that he needs to identify whose fingerprints are on the club. Obviously, he wants to know which are ours and eliminate them."

"You can have them taken at the Saddle River police station," Mike said. "They'll forward them to the Prosecutor's Office."

"We'll go there tomorrow morning," Steve assured him.

Aline put her arm around her mother. "Mom, we all want to see whoever hurt Kerry get caught."

Fran repeated what she had said before. "It was Alan Crowley." Turning to Wilson, she said, "Do you have his fingerprints?"

"Yes, but let's wait for the total fingerprint analysis to be complete."

Aline again walked him to the door. "Mike, I've been thinking and thinking about that text Kerry sent me the day before her party. I say this with love. Kerry had a little bit of the drama queen in her. Whether it was a quarrel with a boyfriend or a dispute with a teacher, she always quickly said what was on her mind. In the text she sent the day before the party she referred to something *very important,* but didn't say what it was. That's not the way Kerry usually did things."

"Aline," Mike said, "I know how hard all this is for you. But I can see that you are a great comfort to your parents."

His hand brushed hers as she opened the door for him. "Aline, I promise you and your mother and father that we are going to find out who did this to Kerry and your family, and that person will go away for a very long time."

"At that time maybe we'll be able to try and put our lives back together," Aline said, but there was doubt in her voice.

28

Bobby, Rich and Stan had collective guilt after lying for Alan. The detective had interviewed them one at a time, and each of them stuck to the story. "Alan got to Nellie's about ten-thirty and left at the same time we did, about eleven-forty-five."

Rich even shared that Alan told them that he was going to see Kerry in the morning and make up with her.

Stan told Mike Wilson that Alan had been mad when he came to Nellie's, but he got over it.

Bobby volunteered that Alan had said that Kerry liked to tease him because she enjoyed making up.

When Mike asked them if they knew who sold the beer to Kerry, they claimed truthfully that they had no idea.

But after they spoke to Mike, they got together and discussed the possibility that Alan might break down and admit that he had left Nellie's early, gone back and killed Kerry.

If Alan did that, what would happen to them? Would they end up in jail for lying?

The three of them, together and individually, worried about that.

They tried to reassure one another but they still had visions of getting arrested and going to jail.

29

Aline was sure she knew why Marge had not brought Jamie to the funeral Mass. From the time Jamie was born, the Chapmans and the Dowlings had been very cordial. Kerry had been Jamie's lifelong friend. How hard it must be for him to comprehend that she's gone forever, Aline thought.

Steve had put in the pool when Kerry was ten. Jamie always wanted to swim in it if Kerry was there. If he was out in the yard, Kerry would call Marge and ask if he could come over to swim. He followed Kerry's every movement in the pool and became a very adequate swimmer himself.

Aline always knew how much he adored Kerry, and how much he would miss her now. When the company came in to close the pool for the winter, she noticed Jamie watching them from his side of the hedge that separated the backyards. Impulsively, she walked over and spoke to him.

"Jamie, how are you?" she asked.

"I'm sad."

"Why are you sad, Jamie?"

"Because Kerry went swimming and then to Heaven."

"I know, Jamie. I'm sad too."

"My daddy went to Heaven, so Kerry is with him."

Jamie's eyes were filling with tears. Aline felt herself on the verge of breaking down. She didn't want to do that in front of him. She said, "I'll see you soon, Jamie," and went back into the house.

30

Mike Wilson decided that his next move would be to go to Nellie's and verify the time that Alan and his friends had been there and when they left. He phoned the restaurant and was told by the manager that the same waitstaff that had been on duty Saturday would be there this evening.

It turned out to be easy to find the waitress he wanted to speak to. Glady Moore had been telling everyone that she had served Alan Crowley the night that poor girl was murdered. Wilson got to the restaurant at seven, spoke to Glady briefly and was told she could take time to talk to him in about fifteen minutes.

The tempting smell of pizza reminded him that he was hungry. He ordered a Margherita pizza and a glass of beer.

As she had promised, Glady came over to his table and sat opposite him. "Kerry used to come in here with her friends," she said.

"She was such a beautiful girl. To think that she was murdered the very night that I was serving pizza to those boys."

"Do you remember what time they got to the restaurant?"

"Three of them, not the boyfriend Alan Crowley, came in around ten o'clock. The Yankees were playing, so they took a table near the bar so they could watch the game."

"When did Alan join them?" Mike asked.

"It was about ten-thirty. You should have seen the look on his face."

"What do you mean by that?" Mike asked.

"He looked so angry. You'd think he wanted to kill somebody. He was so rude to me. He didn't ask for anything. Just pointed to the pizza the other boys were eating, indicating that's what he wanted. Just between you and me, I think he avoided talking because he had been drinking. When I brought his order, he was texting on his cell phone."

"Okay," Mike said. "He arrived at ten-thirty. Let's say you took his order at ten-thirty-five. How long does it take to make the pizza?"

"About ten minutes."

"So you brought him his order at ten-forty-five. What happened next?"

"When he finished it, he just walked out

135

without paying."

"If you can remember, what time was that?"

"Let's see. He talked to the boys for a while. I noticed he was on his phone, texting some more."

"What time do you think it was when he left?"

"I know it was a little after eleven, not later than eleven-fifteen."

"Let's focus on his three friends. Do you remember what time they left?"

"They stayed until the end of the game."

Mike had checked. The game had ended at 11:46.

"Thank you, Glady. You've been very helpful. I may ask you at a later date to come down to my office and give an official statement."

A delighted smile came over Glady's face. "I'd love to. I can make it anytime you want."

As Mike was getting up to leave, he asked, "Did you ever get paid for Alan's pizza?"

"One of his friends took care of it."

Mike went to the Prosecutor's Office, where Assistant Prosecutor Artie Schulman was waiting for him. Artie was the Chief of the Homicide Unit. "Artie, can we talk in my office?" he asked. "It will be easier."

On his wall Mike had a series of whiteboards. The first showed in alphabetical order the names of the kids who had been at Kerry's party. Most of the names were written in black. The seven names written in red were under eighteen years old.

To the left of each name was the date Mike or a member of his team had questioned the student or a big "R." R, Mike explained, meant they refused to be interviewed, or if they were minors, their parents had refused the interview. Eight names were preceded by an "R." To the right of each name was a date in August or September. It was the date of the student's departure for his or her respective college.

On the second whiteboard there were eight names. These were students who claimed they had witnessed the argument that took place between Alan and Kerry at the party. A "T" to the right of their names indicated the girls who had sent a text message to Kerry after the party.

The third whiteboard listed the names of Alan Crowley's three supposed alibi witnesses.

Artie looked at the whiteboards.

"Two of the students who witnessed the arguments are headed for schools in the

Midwest and another is going to California," Mike said. "I'm assuming that for budget reasons, Matt Koenig will want me to complete these interviews in New Jersey versus flying across the country," he added, referring to the County Prosecutor.

"You've got that right," Artie agreed.

Mike updated him on the progress of his investigation. "We got the court order to go through Alan Crowley's cell phone records. He is lying about how long he stayed at the restaurant. His phone pinged a tower right by the victim's home on the other side of Saddle River at 11:25 P.M. It's pretty clear he went back to the victim's home after he left Nellie's."

"What about Crowley's friends who gave him an alibi?"

"It looks like he asked them to lie for him, and they did. I'm going to contact the three of them and have them come down here to give a formal statement. After I read them the riot act about what could happen when you lie to an investigator, I'm sure their memories will improve."

"We've confirmed the golf club was the murder weapon," Schulman said. "Any progress on identifying the fingerprints on it?"

"Yes, but that's going to be a problem,"

Mike told him.

"Why?"

Mike picked up a report on his desk and flipped the page. "According to the lab, there are five separate, identifiable prints on the putter. All of these are on the steel shaft. The numerous prints on the rubber grip are so smudged that they're unusable."

"Anything on the putter head?"

"No."

"So where does that leave us?"

"Alan Crowley's thumbprint is on the putter. The victim's parents, the Dowlings, gave us their prints. Each has one fingerprint on the putter. That leaves two we still have to match."

"Where do we go from there?"

"That is the problem. In my interviews of the party guests, a number of them who spent time outside in the backyard either admitted to using the practice green or gave me the names of boys who were taking turns putting."

"So we have a lot of kids who actually handled the murder weapon?"

"Correct. Of the eight males who I can identify as having handled the putter, not a single one has a criminal record."

"And therefore we don't have their prints on file?"

"Even though most of the students who were at the party consented to be interviewed, I'm pretty sure we'll get a lot of resistance if we ask them to give fingerprints."

Artie nodded. "We can't ask a judge to compel them to give us their prints because they aren't suspects."

"That's right."

"Have you been able to pin down the time of death?" Artie asked.

"The medical examiner's report didn't give us much help there. The pool water was eighty-five degrees. In water that warm, body tissue degrades quickly. The latest we know she was alive was eleven-ten P.M. on Saturday, when she sent her last text. The family found her in the water at eleven-fifteen A.M. on Sunday. So the maximum amount of time she was in the water is about twelve hours."

"So she could have been killed at four in the morning?"

"Yes, but that's highly unlikely. Alan Crowley in his statement said she was going to clean up outside and then go to bed. Her text to him says the same thing. I was at the property. In another ten minutes she could have finished cleaning the backyard."

"So there's no evidence to suggest that

she might have gone to bed and then Crowley forced her to come back outside?"

"No, there isn't. But there *is* evidence that she never went to bed that night. We checked her room. Her bed was made."

"That doesn't tell us much. For all we know, she went to sleep on the couch."

"Agreed. But the autopsy showed that at the time of her death she still had her contact lenses in."

"People forget to take them out, particularly if they've been drinking."

"I spoke to the victim's sister. According to her, Kerry never would have forgotten. One time she left them in overnight and got a serious eye infection. She was religious about taking them out before going to sleep."

"So what time do you think the murder took place?"

"Between eleven-ten, when she sent her last text, and about ten minutes later, when she would have finished cleaning the backyard."

"Precisely the time Crowley came back to the house."

"Artie, I believe that subject to interviewing Crowley's friends who were at Nellie's and confirming that they lied, we have more than enough to arrest Alan Crowley. He was at the party. He was jealous. He sent angry text messages to her. Phone records show that he went back to the home to see her after the party and lied about it. He asked his friends to lie. His fingerprints are on the murder weapon. He denied having touched it the night of the party."

"Where are we on this Good Samaritan flat tire changer?"

"Kerry's friend said Kerry told her that after she picked up the beer, he was aggressive and tried to kiss her. But a couple of her friends say she was a flirt. Maybe she was exaggerating. She was a very pretty young woman. As of today, we've made almost no progress in trying to find him."

"I wish we could have nailed that down, but everything really seems to point to Crowley."

"And we can't talk to Crowley any further because Lester Parker won't allow us."

"All right. Get back to me after you question his three friends. How soon can you talk to them?"

Wilson checked his whiteboard. "One of them is taking a term off. Two of them are in college locally and have agreed to come back. They're coming in to talk to me this afternoon."

31

Bobby, Stan and Rich each received the phone call they dreaded. Detective Mike Wilson told them that the information they had given when they first spoke to him was very important to the investigation. He wanted them to come down to Hackensack and give formal statements. All three had agreed to go to the Prosecutor's Office together at 4:30 that afternoon.

Mike took them into the interrogation room. Normally he interviewed witnesses separately, but he thought it would be more effective to challenge the three of them together. All of them had sweating palms as they sat in the three chairs on one side of the conference table. He turned the video camera on.

Mike began gently. "Alan is your friend, right? You played baseball together."

They all nodded.

"It is very natural for friends to want to

143

help a friend that might be in trouble. I've done it myself. I'm convinced that is what each of you did the last time I spoke to you. Well, things are different today. I know a lot more about what happened that night and who was where at what time. So I'm going to ask you questions. This is your chance to put things right. If you lie to me today, you will be charged with false swearing and obstruction of justice." Mike paused. "And possibly accessory to murder. Now, let's get started."

Words tumbled out of the mouths of all three of them. "Alan left Nellie's before we did. We didn't know we'd be in trouble. When Alan phoned, he sounded so scared. The minute we lied for him, we knew we were making a mistake."

Mike said, "Okay, hold on. What time did Alan leave Nellie's?"

Desperate to be exact, the three of them agreed it was about eleven-fifteen.

Mike asked, "Did he say anything about where he was going?"

Stan answered, "Kerry had sent him a text telling him not to come over until tomorrow. But he said he wanted to straighten things out that night."

Mike said, "So it was your impression that he was leaving Nellie's and going directly to

Kerry's?"

"Yes."

"When Alan joined you at Nellie's, can you tell me if he had been drinking?"

There was a moment of silence. Then all three nodded.

"A little? A lot? How much?"

"He was kinda drunk when he got to Nellie's, but after he had the pizza and soda, he was pretty okay," Rich said.

The three affirmed that they were together at Stan's pool that Sunday afternoon when Alan phoned and asked them to lie for him.

"I thank you for coming here today. You did the right thing by telling us the truth."

Watching them leave, Mike thought that nobody had ever been happier to get out of here than these three.

He went back to his office and called Artie. They agreed that it was time to arrest Alan Crowley.

32

June and Doug Crowley felt somewhat relieved after their meeting with Lester Parker. They drove directly home with Alan. When they were inside, June went into the den and settled there with a satisfied sigh. Doug and Alan followed her in.

"Lester Parker may be expensive, but I believe he's worth it," June observed. Her expression changed. "Fran Dowling is telling everyone that you killed Kerry," she said, looking at Alan. "I'm going to have Parker write a stiff letter to her saying that we are going to sue her if she continues her malicious defamation."

"I agree," Doug said heartily.

They both looked at Alan, expecting his approval.

"Mom, Dad, there's something I have to tell you."

Oh my God, he's going to tell us he killed her, June thought, her blood running cold.

"I wasn't honest with you or the detective in Hackensack about where I was after I left the party. I did go to Nellie's, but on my way home, I went to Kerry's house."

"Alan, don't tell us you killed her," June begged.

A suddenly white-faced Doug gripped the arms of the chair, preparing for the worst.

"I killed her? That's what you two have believed all along!" Alan snapped. "Here's what really happened. I went back to make up with Kerry and help her clean up. We spoke for a few minutes. She told me she was tired and going to bed, she said she would get up early in the morning to clean up. I kissed her good night and came straight home."

"Then why did you lie to the detective?" Doug asked.

"Because I knew it would look bad for me. We had a fight at the party and everybody saw it. I sent her some nasty text messages which I'm sure the cops know about. If I admitted going back to her house, I was afraid how that would look."

"Alan," June said, "you know your father and I are behind you no matter what."

"No matter what! What does that mean? You're behind me even if I killed her?" Alan stood up. "Well you might as well know I not only lied to the detective. I asked my friends to lie and say I was at Nellie's with them when I was really at Kerry's."

Doug and June were too stunned to react. Alan looked at his mother. "You better not send that letter to Mrs. Dowling," he said bitterly, and stalked out of the room.

33

Brenda was in the kitchen when she heard raised voices coming from the den. Knowing every inch of the house and blessed with exceptionally good hearing, she knew exactly where to go when she wanted to listen to Crowley conversations. She tiptoed from the kitchen down the hall and ducked into the small bathroom next to the den. She brought a roll of paper towels and a bottle of Windex in case she had to look busy.

The words "He lied to the detective" swirled around in her brain. Always sympathetic to Alan because of the Crowleys' demands on him, she began to wonder. Why would he have lied to the cops? There's no way he would hurt Kerry.

She couldn't wait to get over to talk to Marge after she finished preparing dinner for the Crowleys.

She was glad to see Marge's car as she drove up her street. When Marge answered the door and invited her in, she pointed up the stairs. "Brenda, Jamie's having a really bad day. He's been crying because he misses Kerry," she said, her tone weary.

"Oh, Marge, I'm so sorry."

"It happens every few days. He misses her so much. I think losing Kerry is bringing back his sadness from when Jack died."

"Of course, he misses Kerry and his father," Brenda said sympathetically. "But wait till you hear the latest."

She waited until they were seated at the kitchen table and Marge had put on the kettle for a cup of tea. "Marge," Brenda began, "you won't believe me when I tell you what Alan told the Crowleys!"

34

At six-forty-five the next morning, Fran and Steve were awakened by the ringing of the bedside phone. Fran groped for it and sat up straight. It was Mike Wilson telling her that they were on their way to arrest Alan Crowley for Kerry's murder. He would be brought to the Bergen County Jail in Hackensack today and would be arraigned in the next couple days. The arraignment before the judge would be open to the public, and the Dowlings could attend.

Mike added, "Mrs. Dowling, we'll be there in a few minutes. Do not share this information until I've called you back to confirm that Alan was at his house and is in our custody."

Fran replaced the phone and said, "Steve, fantastic news! It's just as I've been saying. Alan Crowley is being arrested today for killing Kerry."

Fifteen minutes later, June and Doug

Crowley were startled awake by persistent pounding on their front door and the ringing of the doorbell. Instinctively suspecting that the reason for the abrupt intrusion was going to be a problem, June grabbed her robe and raced downstairs.

She yanked open the door and saw two men in plainclothes side by side with a uniformed policeman. She had no way of knowing that another uniformed officer was in the backyard to guard against the possibility that Alan would try to escape.

"Ma'am, I'm Detective Wilson from the Bergen County Prosecutor's Office. We have a warrant for the arrest of Alan Crowley and a search warrant for the premises," he told her. "Is he here at this time?"

"My son is represented by counsel, by Lester Parker. Have you spoken to him?"

"Your son has the right to speak to his attorney later. We are here now to arrest him."

Without being asked, Wilson pushed open the door and stepped past June Crowley into the house. His fellow detective and the officer followed him.

By this time Doug and Alan were tumbling down the stairs in time to hear the word "arrest." Alan gripped his father's arm as the words sank in. He was dressed in only a T-shirt and boxers.

He looked at Mike Wilson. "Can I at least get dressed?"

Wilson answered Alan's question. "Yes, you can get dressed. We'll follow you to your room."

He and the other detective climbed the stairs behind Alan and walked down the hallway to his room. Two partially packed suitcases were on the floor by the window. Next to them was an unzipped Nike sports bag with several wooden bats and two baseball gloves inside.

"Are you going someplace, Alan?" Mike asked, although he already knew the answer.

"I'm leaving for college the day after tomorrow," Alan said. "Can I still go?"

"Let's see how today goes," Mike said matter-of-factly.

He watched as Alan went into his closet and pulled out jeans and a pair of running shoes.

"Sorry, Alan. No shoelaces, no belt and no jewelry."

In her bedroom June was frantically dialing Lester Parker's office. Filled with frustration at being connected to a recording, she shrieked, "This is June Crowley. The police are here with a warrant for Alan's arrest. Call me on my cell phone at once." She reached into her closet and grabbed a running suit.

Doug was quickly pulling on a pair of pants and shirt. They managed to be back downstairs as Alan, a detective on each side of him, was walking out the front door toward the waiting cars.

"Where are you taking him?" June shouted. She gasped as she noticed for the first time that Alan's hands were cuffed behind his back.

Mike answered, "To the Bergen County Jail in Hackensack."

June saw two of her neighbors standing in their driveways observing the scene that was unfolding before them.

"Can one of us ride with Alan?" she yelled to Mike Wilson.

"No, but you can follow us to the jail."

June jogged to catch up to them. She grabbed Alan's arm as Wilson was opening the back door of his unmarked car. "Alan, I phoned Lester Parker. He's going to get right back to me. Remember what he told you. Don't answer any questions unless he is with you."

There were tears in Alan's eyes. Before he had a chance to answer her, he felt Wilson's hand on his head firmly forcing it down as he slid through the opened door. There was a wire grill separating the front and back seats.

June maintained eye contact with Alan for as long as she could as the car began to slowly back down her driveway. As she watched Wilson drive away, her normally steely resolve melted. "My baby, oh my God, my baby," she sobbed as Doug put his arm around her and helped her toward his car.

After turning off Hollywood Avenue, the detective's car accelerated onto Route 17. The traffic was moving quickly as they were a little ahead of the worst part of the morning rush.

A bewildered Alan tried to make sense of what was going on around him. Only days ago, he had ridden in this same car with Detective Wilson, to Hackensack. But on the earlier trip he had been in the front seat and was not wearing handcuffs. He found himself hoping that this was one long nightmare. When he woke up, he would go to Kerry's house, make up with her and hurry home to mow the lawn. And finish organizing what he would bring to college. It didn't work. This was real.

Wilson and the other detective made no attempt to speak to him. He could hear them talking about the monstrously long home run the Yankees' Aaron Judge had hit the previous evening. He had seen it. For them this is just another day at the office, he thought. For me, my life is over.

Processing at the jail was a blur. The bright flashes as he was photographed straight on and in profile. Being fingerprinted again. Answering a barrage of questions.

Alan was taken into a windowless room. His handcuffs were removed. He was given a bag and told to take off his clothes and put them in it. He assumed it would be okay to keep his underwear on. He was told to put on an orange jumpsuit that was on the counter in front of him.

After changing, he was taken to a community holding cell. About a dozen people were there. There were benches along the walls of the room and one in the center. Toward the back of the cell on the right, in full view of all, was a stainless steel toilet. No one was sitting on the bench closest to it. Alan took a seat on a bench near the cell door.

About half the people in the cell appeared to be around his age or a little older. One prisoner sitting by himself in the corner smelled to high heaven. Everybody was sitting, most with their heads down. There were a few conversations going on. A loud-mouth was sharing his experiences with someone who had never been arrested. Alan heard another one explaining the difference between jail and prison. "If you incarcerated for up to 364 days, you in jail; 365 days or more, you in prison."

Alan had not eaten breakfast and was very hungry. He made eye contact with a middle-aged man on the bench opposite him. "Is food something you ask for, or do they bring it when they're ready?"

The man smiled. "They just bring it, but believe me, it's nothing you'd ask for."

There was no clock that he could see, and watches weren't permitted. After what he thought was several hours, a guard began unlocking the cell door. Behind the guard was an older man pushing a cart with numerous paper bags on the top tray. Alan was handed a brown paper bag. Inside was something wrapped in wax paper. He put it on his lap and opened it. The thickness of the stale roll covered the two slices of baloney deep inside. He assumed the gooey white substance was mayonnaise.

The man opposite him had seen the expression on his face. "I guess they were out of filet mignon," he said as he bit into his sandwich.

Fearful that dinner would not be any better, Alan forced himself to eat half of it. Also in the bag, compliments of the state of New Jersey, was a plastic bottle of water.

He was later moved to the commons area in the general population. About twenty inmates were seated on folding chairs watching CNN. Small groups were off to the sides playing chess, checkers and cards. Recreation time, Alan thought bitterly.

In the late afternoon they were marched into what passed for a dining room. He followed the lead of others who took a tray and a plate and walked past the servers who put scoops on their plates. The utensils were plastic.

He spotted a half-filled table where the inmates appeared to be near his age. They were exchanging stories about why they had been arrested. Two of them had been caught with heroin. Another was serving a drunk driving sentence, his third. They looked at him, obviously expecting to hear his story. "My girlfriend died in an accident. They're blaming me."

"Which judge you got?"

"I don't know."

After dinner they were herded back to the community room. One of the inmates who had been at the dinner table asked Alan, "You play chess?"

"Yeah, I do," he said as he followed the other prisoner to a table. In the time he had been in the jail, it was the only hour that passed relatively quickly.

A few minutes after the game ended, the prisoners stood up and formed a queue along the wall. "Back to the cells," Alan's chess opponent announced. "See you tomorrow."

The guard unlocked a cell and directed him into it. There were bunk beds along the left wall. A stainless steel toilet was in the right corner. A very small window overlooked the parking area behind the courthouse.

A man who appeared to be in his thirties, in the lower bunk, glanced at him as he came in, but then went back to whatever he was reading. Alan wanted to find out where he could get something to read, but he was too nervous to ask.

The top bunk was his, but Alan was uncertain about what to do. There was no ladder. In order to hoist himself up, he would have to put one foot on the lower bunk. Should I ask permission or just do it?

Better not to disturb him, Alan thought as he put a foot on the lower end of the bottom bunk and vaulted himself to the top. He waited apprehensively for a protest from below. There was none.

The mattress was thin and lumpy. The blanket and sheet had a strong smell of disinfectant.

Alan put his hands behind his head on the small pillow and stared at the ceiling. It was several hours before he fell asleep. It was a challenge to tune out the loud snoring emanating from the bunk beneath him.

He was startled awake by the sound of voices, footsteps and cell doors sliding open. Following a line of prisoners, he went to the same room where he had had dinner the previous evening, this time for breakfast.

He had just followed the procession to the recreation room when a guard barked, "Alan Crowley."

Alan meekly raised his hand. "Let's go," the guard said, gesturing him to follow. He was led down a long corridor with doors on each side. Above each door was a plate that read ATTORNEY-CLIENT ROOM followed by a number. The guard opened the door to number 7. Alan spotted Lester Parker seated at the table, with his briefcase next to him. He took a chair opposite him.

"Alan, how are you doing?" Parker said as they shook hands.

"I'm undefeated in chess," Alan said wryly.

Parker smiled. "I've spoken to the assistant prosecutor. We went over the charges against you. They'll bring you into court tomorrow at eleven. I'll be there."

"After court tomorrow, will I be getting out of here?"

"I can't say with certainty what's going to happen tomorrow, but I'm going to make a strong argument that you be allowed to go home."

"Will my parents be there, in court?"

"Yes, and they want you home just as much as you want to go home. I'll see you tomorrow. And remember, talk to no one about your case."

35

Word of Alan Crowley's arrest had begun to spread in the afternoon. Aline saw students in their breaks between classes, at their lockers, staring down at their phones. NorthJersey.com had been the first to report the story. She picked up her phone, but then decided against calling her mother.

When she drove up the driveway a few minutes before six that evening, Steve pulled in right behind her. When they were both out of their cars, she said, "I am sure that Alan's arrest will be on the television news tonight."

Steve nodded. "Yes. I was thinking the same thing."

As he opened the front door, Steve called, "Fran."

"In here."

Steve and Aline went to the den, where Fran had the TV on Channel 2. They watched in silence as the segment that had been on the five o'clock news was repeated.

Steve moved quickly to where Fran was sitting and put his arm around her. "Are you okay?" he asked.

"Yes," she said. "In fact I'm . . ." She paused. " 'Glad' is not the right word. I'll never have real peace, but when Alan goes to prison, I'll have some sense that justice has been served."

"Mom," Aline said, "remember, Alan's only been accused of the crime. That doesn't mean —"

Steve interrupted her. "They usually don't arrest somebody until they've got the right guy and have enough to convict him."

"Aline, why are you defending him?" Fran snapped. "He killed your sister, and then he lied about it."

"Mom, Dad, please," Aline said. "I'm not trying to start a fight. When Kerry and Alan were going out, they were constantly quarreling, breaking up and then getting back together. They repeated that cycle a bunch of times. But after they quarrel at Kerry's party, this time he comes back to the house and kills her? I don't know. It just doesn't add up."

"What doesn't add up?" Fran said heatedly. "You know he lied about coming back to the house after the party."

"I understand that, but listen to me. Kids who are barely eighteen are incredibly insecure. I work with them every day. They think they're adults, but they're not. When you confront them, they look for the easy way out, even if that means lying," Aline said, her voice rising. "I'd be really nervous if a cop showed up today and took me in for questioning. I can only imagine how panicky I would have been ten years ago when I was eighteen."

Fran was having none of it. "You can rationalize this as much as you want. I don't care if he was a scared young kid. Alan Crowley killed Kerry, and he's going to pay for it."

"Fran, Aline," Steve interrupted, "the last thing we need to do is quarrel with each other. The truth will come out at the trial."

Fran had the last word. "At the trial when he's found guilty, you mean."

36

Alan was taken from the jail and escorted into the adjacent courthouse, where he appeared before a judge at about 11:30 A.M. The guards seated him next to a waiting Lester Parker.

His parents sat on one side of the courtroom, in the first row of the spectator seats. His mother gasped when she saw him in the orange jumpsuit. This time his hands were cuffed in front of him.

On the other side of the courtroom, in the front row, were Fran and Steve Dowling. When they made eye contact with him, he turned away.

The assistant prosecutor read the charges against him. Murder, possession of a weapon for an unlawful purpose — the golf club — and tampering with witnesses. The judge, a balding man with glasses pushed high on his forehead, turned to Lester Parker. "Counsel, how does your client plead?"

"Not guilty, Your Honor."

Turning to the assistant prosecutor, the judge stated, "Your Office has moved to detain the defendant pending trial."

The assistant prosecutor began, "Your Honor, the State has a very strong case against Alan Crowley. Our investigation has revealed that he attended a party at the home of Kerry Dowling the night of her death and became extremely jealous when another young man spoke to her. We allege that later in the evening, after everyone else was gone, he returned and struck her in the back of the head with a golf club. She fell into the pool in the backyard of her home. Her family discovered her body in the pool the next morning. He lied to a detective regarding his whereabouts at the time of the crime and induced several friends to lie on his behalf. They have since admitted that they lied. He also lied about handling the golf club that evening, but it has his fingerprint on it."

The assistant prosecutor continued. "Your Honor, we are seriously concerned about the risk of flight if he were released. He faces life in prison. He has already tampered with witnesses and could seek to do so again."

Alan lowered his head and closed his eyes

as he listened to the evil picture painted of him.

Parker's response was loud and forceful. "Your Honor, my client has no record of any kind. He hasn't even had a traffic ticket. He has no history whatsoever of violence. He has lived in the same house in Saddle River with his parents since he was born. He is their only child. He graduated from high school three months ago and is scheduled to begin college at Princeton within a few days. He has absolutely no resources of his own."

Parker continued, "Your Honor, I have been provided with some of the investigative reports. The prosecutor failed to mention that there were no witnesses to the crime. He also failed to mention that there are at least two other unidentified fingerprints on the golf club. One of those fingerprints may belong to the perpetrator of this terrible crime.

"The reports also indicate that Kerry had had an encounter with a young man who had very recently stopped to help her change a flat tire. The victim told friends that this young man had bought the alcohol for her party but had become angry and aggressive with her when she declined his request to be invited to the party. This person has never been identified but should be considered a person of considerable interest in this investigation.

"Your Honor, we no longer have a bail system. You either detain the defendant or you don't. It would be a travesty for him to spend a year or more in jail awaiting trial. We intend to vigorously defend against these charges. The State has no basis whatsoever for considering him to be a threat to anyone in the community or a flight risk."

Solemnly, the judge reflected upon the arguments. "This is a difficult decision. The defendant is charged with a heinous crime. I consider most carefully the prosecutor's arguments in support of detention. But defense counsel has also offered strong arguments. The defendant is eighteen years old. I do not believe he is a strong risk of flight. There is no evidence that he represents a threat to any specific person in the community. Counsel has argued that there are no witnesses to this crime and the evidence is circumstantial. Under all of these circumstances, I am entering the following order.

"The defendant is released under the following conditions. He is to wear an electronic monitoring bracelet at all times. He may not leave the state of New Jersey without the permission of this court. He is to live at his parents' Saddle River address unless he is at college, which I note is in the state of New Jersey. He is to have no contact with the victim's family.

"The defendant shall be taken back to the Bergen County Jail, where he will be fitted with the electronic bracelet and thereafter be released."

Alan's shoulders visibly slumped in relief. Parker put his arm on his shoulder and whispered, "Okay, Alan. Go home and get some rest. I will call you tomorrow. Remember, aside from your parents, talk to no one about your case."

To avoid an encounter between the families, the Sheriff's Department allowed the Dowling family to leave first. Once they were on the elevator, the Crowleys got up to go.

37

A distraught and angry June Crowley drove home with Doug and Alan. It had taken nearly two hours after the arraignment to have Alan returned to the Bergen County Jail and then processed out. On the way to Saddle River, Alan closed his eyes as though he were asleep. There was zero conversation during the twenty-five-minute ride. They were all hungry. Doug and June had barely had any breakfast, and except for cups of coffee at the courthouse, they hadn't eaten since early morning. Alan had been so nervous before the arraignment that he hadn't eaten a bite of the jail breakfast.

Together they walked into the kitchen and were glad to see that Brenda had an early dinner prepared. As usual, she had the small kitchen TV on while she worked. They all froze when they heard the name "Crowley" and looked up at the set. On screen was Alan, handcuffed and in the orange jumpsuit, being led into the courthouse. The reporter was saying, "Alan Crowley, the boyfriend of murdered teen Kerry Dowling, was in court this morning.

"He was arraigned before Judge Paul Martinez on charges of murder, possession of a weapon for an unlawful purpose, and witness tampering. He pleaded not guilty. After being fitted with an electronic bracelet, he was released into the custody of his parents.

"June Crowley, the mother of the accused, spoke to me on camera after the arraignment."

"There is no way in the world my son committed this crime. He loved Kerry. The only reason he went back to her house the night of her party was to help her clean up and make sure she was all right. The police scared the hell out of a kid who had just turned eighteen. They snatched him from our home on a Sunday morning when my husband and I were not home, drove him to the Prosecutor's Office, interrogated him and intimidated him into lying. And now they're saying because he lied, he must have killed her."

She was interrupted by a visibly annoyed Lester Parker, who took June's arm and physically moved her away from the microphone. He stated firmly, "A vigorous defense will be mounted on behalf of Alan Crowley. When all the facts are known, he will be vindicated. There will be no further statements from the Crowleys before the trial."

An awkward silence followed when the news station moved on to the next story.

Brenda said, "The meatloaf, vegetables and potatoes just need to be warmed." She gave Alan a sympathetic smile. "I'll let you eat in peace," she said as she hurried toward the door.

38

Marge and Jamie were having dinner in the kitchen when Marge turned on the television to get the six o'clock news. The lead story was the arraignment of Alan Crowley. She watched as Alan, pale and tense, left the courthouse with photographers and reporters chasing after him.

"That's Alan Crowley," Jamie said.

"I didn't know you knew Alan," Marge said.

"He's Kerry's friend, before she went to Heaven."

"Yes, he is."

"He kisses her."

"Yes, he does," Marge said.

"He kissed her before she went swimming and went to Heaven."

"Jamie, are you talking about the night of Kerry's party, when you went swimming with her?"

"I promised not to talk about that."

"This time it's okay, Jamie. What did Alan do after he kissed Kerry?"

"He gave her a hug and went home."

"Then what happened, Jamie?"

"The Big Guy hit Kerry and he pushed her in the pool."

"Jamie, are you sure?"

"Cross my heart. Daddy used to call me Big Guy, right, Mom?"

"Yes, Jamie, that's right. But remember, we don't talk to anybody about what happened the night Kerry went to Heaven. That's our secret."

"Cross my heart, Mom. I didn't tell anyone."

Following his usual routine, after dinner Jamie went upstairs to watch television. Heavy hearted, Marge stayed at the kitchen table and made herself another pot of tea. She was starkly aware of what Jamie had told her. If Jamie was describing what he saw the night Kerry was killed, then Kerry was still alive when Alan left. Might Alan have come back and killed Kerry? I guess that's possible, she thought, but why would he do that? The Big Guy Jamie is referring to clearly is not Alan. But who is it?

If Jamie talks about the Big Guy to the detective, and Jamie tells him Jack used to call him the Big Guy, they might assume he was talking about himself. I can only imagine how the Crowleys are feeling right now. How would I feel if Jamie got arrested? He'd be so frightened. I don't know what to do. I just don't know what to do.

39

Detective Mike Wilson had not been able to put his mind at rest. He was deeply distressed that he had not been to able tie up a troubling loose end in the investigation.

He had virtually no information that would lead them to the man who had sold Kerry the beer and then tried to force himself on her. According to Kerry's friend who had told him about the incident, he had suggested meeting Kerry at her house after the party was over.

Suppose he had come over after Alan left. He had already been aggressive with Kerry. If she refused him again, might he have become violent?

There was one way they might possibly get a lead on him.

The next day Mike called Aline at work. "Aline, even though Alan has been charged, I still need to do a few things to complete the investigation, and you might be able to help me."

"Of course," Aline said.

"I'd like to meet and talk to you quietly for a few minutes."

"Sure. Do you want to come to the house?"

"No. This is a conversation I would rather have with you alone."

"When do you have in mind?"

"By any chance are you free tonight?"

"Yes, I am."

"I'd like to get a little away from Saddle River, where we both could be recognized."

They agreed to meet at a diner on Old Hook Road in Westwood.

When Aline arrived promptly at 5:30, Mike waved to her from the corner booth. She slid in opposite him.

"After I spoke to you, it occurred to me that you'd probably prefer to go to a place for a glass of wine versus a cup of coffee," he said.

"To be honest, that would have been my first choice. As it is, I drink too much coffee."

Mike smiled. "Aline, the next building over is an Irish pub that just opened. We wouldn't even have to move our cars. Do you want to walk over there?"

"Sounds great to me."

Five minutes later they were sitting in O'Malley's, at a table in the corner of the bar. Aline took her first sip of Pinot Grigio while Mike took a drink from his beer.

"Aline, I know how strongly your mother feels about Alan Crowley's guilt, which is why I don't want to have this discussion in her presence. I do believe that he did it, but there are two loose ends that I wish I could clear up. The first is to find whoever helped Kerry with the tire."

"Is there any way I can help you with that?"

"Seven girls who were at the party are still seniors at the high school. They're minors. These parents refused to allow them to talk to me. In your work as a guidance counselor, I assume you're going to interact with some of these girls."

"At some point I probably will."

"It makes sense that they might want to talk to you about Kerry."

"Possibly."

"Kerry told one girl about the guy who helped her with the tire. She might have told some of these girls as well. If they talk to you about Kerry, could you somehow work that into the conversation?"

Aline exhaled. "You must know I'm on really shaky ethical ground here. The privacy rules for guidance counselors are very strict."

"I understand that. I'm not looking for personal information on these girls. Maybe I don't even have to know the name of the girl who shares something with you. But if any of them knows something that will lead me to that guy, it will be enormously helpful. If I give you a list of their names, could you get them to talk about Kerry and bring up the subject of the guy who helped her with the tire?"

Aline considered for a minute. Once again, she knew that she would be taking a chance on losing her job. On the other hand she had seen the disbelieving look on Alan Crowley's face when he had been photographed leaving the courtroom in prison clothes and handcuffs. If there was even the slightest chance that he was innocent . . .

"I'll do it," she said firmly.

Mike's serious expression brightened.

"Thank you. It's a lead that may not go anywhere, but I need to follow it through."

He picked up the stein of beer on the table in front of him. "A glass of beer hits the spot at the end of the day," he said.

"And so does a glass of wine."

He leaned his glass forward. "A toast to that."

They clinked glasses.

"You said there was something else you wanted to talk to me about." Aline's tone of voice was more of a question.

"It may be nothing, but that last text Kerry sent you the day of the party sticks in my mind. You had said she was something of a drama queen, but I wonder if you've had any ideas about what she might have been referring to."

"I've asked myself the same thing over and over," Aline said slowly. "The answer is no. Kerry would write something like, got A's in two classes . . . celebrating that our team won three games in a row. But never anything like 'something *very important* to talk to you about.' "

"Aline, from my interviews I have learned that Kerry and Alan would break up and then get back together the next day. Do you think there's any chance that the text was referring to him?"

Aline shook her head. "The answer is I simply don't know."

"I thought you'd say that."

Mike took a sip from the beer. "What I'm asking you to do is to encourage those girls to talk to you about Kerry, ask if she told any of them what was so *very important.*"

This time Aline did not hesitate. "Yes to

that request too."

"Then we're on the same page." Mike paused then added, "I'm getting hungry. Any chance you might stay for dinner? I just came upon this place last month. Wherever they found the chef, he's excellent."

That's the second dinner invitation in a few days, Aline thought.

Her parents were having dinner with friends at the club. Why not? Aline asked herself. "I hope they have corned beef and cabbage," she told Mike.

"That's a must when you're an Irish pub. I had it last week. It's really good."

"You've convinced me."

The dinner was as good as Mike had promised. They compared their backgrounds. Aline said, "I went to Columbia. I always thought I would be a social worker or a teacher. But when I was studying for my master's, I decided that being a guidance counselor would be the right fit for me. I really enjoy helping the kids with their choices."

"I'm a local guy too. I grew up in Washington Township, played football at St. Joe's in Montvale and went to Michigan. No, I didn't play football there."

"Are your parents, family, still in Washington Township?"

"I'm an only child and no, right after I graduated high school, my parents moved to New York City. Dad walks to his law office and Mom loves being closer to the arts."

"And what did you do after you finished Michigan?"

"After I graduated, I realized I wanted to work in criminal justice. I got a master's at John Jay in Manhattan. I was on the police force in Waldwick for a couple years before I got the position in the Prosecutor's Office. This past June I finished a grueling four years of going to Seton Hall Law School at night."

"You sound very ambitious. What are you going to do with your law degree?"

"The first thing I'm going to do is try to pass the bar exam. After that, I'm not sure. But if I want to move up the ladder in police work, having a law degree will be very helpful."

"Have you worked with families like mine, where a family member was murdered?"

"In the six years I've been at the Prosecutor's Office, unfortunately, many times."

"As a guidance counselor, I'm supposed to be a bit of an expert on coping strategies. I know how bad it is for me, but I can see that my father and mother are torn apart. I wonder if anything will ever bring them peace."

"When the trial is over and justice has been served, that's when the real healing will start."

"I hope so," Aline said. "They certainly helped me when I was going through hell."

At the query on Mike's face, she told him about losing Rick to a drunk driver.

"What happened to the driver who killed him?"

"He was found not guilty because a friend lied for him. Nobody saw the accident. We really believe that his passenger, who was his friend and who hadn't been drinking, switched places with him before the police arrived. Other witnesses who were at the party said that when he left, and this was just a few minutes before the accident, he had been drinking heavily and he had been driving. And it was *his* car. But I guess the jury just wasn't sure, and they let him off."

"Sometimes those things happen."

Aline hesitated and then said, her voice quivering, "Right now he's married, has two kids and a good job on Wall Street, and is living happily ever after."

"How have you been able to cope with that?" Mike asked gently.

"At first, I was terribly angry and resentful. That was why I took the job in London, at the International School. I wanted to get away. For a long time I was completely bitter. But one day I woke up and realized I was ruining my life by not accepting what happened. And then I realized my being angry and bitter wasn't going to change anything. As hard and unfair as things can be, I had to move on or else I'd go crazy."

"I'm glad you made that choice. I'm sure that's what your fiancé would have wanted you to do."

"I agree." For a moment Aline was lost in thought. Then her expression brightened. "I just realized something. I was sure you looked familiar the first time I saw you at my parents' house. In my freshman year in high school my girlfriends and I went to see the spring play at St. Joe's. They were doing *West Side Story.* By any chance were you in it?"

"I've just met a girl named Mah-REEE-ahh," Mike began to sing softly.

"It was you! I love that song. You were so good. I'm a pretty good soprano. I'd sing it along with you, but I don't want us to get thrown out of the bar."

"If they don't like that one, we could do 'Danny Boy' instead."

Aline laughed, a genuine laugh. It made

her realize it was the first time she had felt really good in a long time.

40

The morning after his arraignment Alan woke up groggy with sleep. He had had a vivid dream involving Kerry and the last minutes he was with her. For a moment he had hesitated after he walked around the house. Kissing her goodbye. The funeral. Kerry asking him, "Alan, why are you wearing handcuffs?" Reporters. Questions shouted at him.

When he opened his eyes, it was 7:45. As his brain cleared, the reality of what had happened leapt into his mind. What will happen next? I'm supposed to go to Princeton tomorrow.

He looked across the room at his half-packed suitcase. Will I be able to finish packing? he wondered as he headed for the shower.

When he went downstairs, his mother and father were sitting at the kitchen table having coffee. They both looked as though they'd had a lousy night's sleep. Worrying about me, of course, he thought bitterly. His father's laptop was open in front of him.

Looking up from the computer, he greeted him with a question. "Alan, have you checked your email this morning?"

"No, why?"

His mother and father looked at each other. She said, "Alan, your father and I received an email from Princeton. You were copied on it. It was from the dean of admissions. They urgently need to schedule a teleconference with the three of us today."

"Today?" Alan said. "So that means they want to talk to us before we drive down there tomorrow. They're probably going to say they changed their minds and are rejecting me."

"Alan," his father said, "let's not get ahead of ourselves. I replied that we will speak to them at nine this morning."

"Should we ask Lester Parker if he should be on the call?" June asked.

"Let's see what they have to say before we start getting lawyers involved," Doug said.

Alan was sure he would not be driving to Princeton tomorrow. He did not voice that to his mother or father, although he could tell from their faces that that was what they thought too. He remembered how they had hammered into him the need to have good marks. All because they believed graduating from an Ivy League school sets you up for life. Now Princeton is going to tell him to stay home.

His mother suggested making him French toast, his favorite. Her tone reminded him of the time she offered him ice cream after he had his tonsils out. Despite everything, he was hungry.

"Okay, thanks," he said.

They had breakfast in complete silence. At one minute before nine, his father dialed into the teleconference number provided in the email. He put the phone on speaker.

David Willis introduced himself as Princeton's director of admissions. "I also have on the call with me Lawrence Knolls, chief counsel to Princeton University."

Perfunctory greetings were exchanged before Willis came to the point.

"Alan, we are aware of the unfortunate circumstances in which you find yourself. We have come to the conclusion that it would be in the best interest of all parties if you were to defer enrollment until your personal situation is satisfactorily resolved."

June said, "But we are planning to drive him for freshman registration tomorrow."

"I know that Mrs. Crowley. That is why

we are speaking today."

Doug jumped in. "You said, '*if* you were to defer enrollment.' Is this Alan's choice, or are you telling us this is what he has to do?"

"I'm sorry if I was not clear. It would be awkward under the present circumstances for Alan to take his place in the freshman class."

"What is that supposed to mean?" June demanded.

This time it was the attorney who responded. "It means when all of the charges against Alan have been dismissed, he can apply for readmission."

"I told you we should have had Lester Parker on this call," June interrupted, glaring at Doug.

"We will refund to you the money you have sent to date," Willis added.

Alan asked, "How did you find out about what happened to me?"

Lawrence Knolls answered, "We make an effort to keep track of our incoming freshmen, but I will not answer more specifically than that."

When the call ended, Knolls dialed Willis, who picked up immediately. He said, "David, I guess that went as well as could be expected."

"Do you think they'll challenge our decision?"

"I doubt it. Any lawyer who reviews our terms of acceptance will see that our moral turpitude clause gives us wide latitude regarding whom we allow to enroll."

"By the way," Willis added, "our news monitoring service appears to have worked. I got an email from the PR firm this morning. They attached the article from a northern New Jersey paper about 'Princeton-bound' Alan Crowley being arrested for murder."

"Well, that's reassuring that they picked it up," Knolls said.

"Yes, it is," Willis agreed.

In this case the monitoring service had not been necessary. Two calls about Alan Crowley had already been made to the university's Office of Admissions. The first was polite, almost apologetic. The second was a very angry caller who questioned the type of student Princeton was admitting nowadays.

41

As the days passed, Marge became more and more concerned about Jamie. Usually sunny in the morning and looking forward to going to work, he had become very silent. In her attempts at conversation, he invariably brought up Kerry's name. "Kerry's in Heaven with Daddy. I want to go there too."

"You will someday, but not for a long time. I need you here with me, Jamie."

"You can come up with us too."

Another time out of the blue he asked, "In Heaven, do people go swimming like Kerry did?"

"Maybe." Dear God, please don't let him keep bringing up Kerry's name, Marge begged. She tried to change the subject. "Now that football has started again, are you looking forward to going and watching the practices?"

"They're big guys too."

"Does anyone call you Big Guy, Jamie?"

"Daddy did."

"I know. Anybody else?"

Jamie smiled. "I call myself the Big Guy."

Despairing, Marge thought, It's only a matter of time before he talks to somebody and gets himself in trouble.

42

Aline began to fall into the welcome pattern of busy days at school. True to her promise to Mike, she tried to make a point of meeting the seven girls who had been at the party but had not spoken to the police. She was making slow progress before help came from an unexpected source, Pat Tarleton, who stopped into her office one morning.

"Good morning, Aline. How are things at home?"

Aline sighed. "Okay, I guess."

"Anything wrong?" Pat asked.

"Last night at dinner my mother and I got into a," she paused, "let's say we had a frank exchange of viewpoints."

"Uh-oh, about what?"

"Mom told us that she called Princeton to give them a piece of her mind and let them know what she thought of the type of students they are admitting. Of course, she was referring to Alan Crowley. I told her I thought that she was wrong. He has only been accused of a crime. He hasn't been convicted. I told her she should stay out of it. Needless to say, she strongly disagreed."

"Oh, Aline, I'm sorry."

"It's all right, Pat. We're back on speaking terms."

"No, Aline. I'm sorry I didn't tell you *I* called Princeton to make sure they knew about Alan's arrest."

"Pat, I don't understand. Why would you —"

"Because Aline, I have a duty to this school and our current and future students. Every parent in this town is hoping their son or daughter will be accepted by Ivy League schools or the Notre Dames and Georgetowns. As you well know, the competition to get into these places is fierce. It is essential that Saddle River High maintain a good relationship with them, including Princeton. If we didn't give them a heads-up that one of our students who is headed their way was going to cause them bad publicity, they could make it that much tougher for future students who apply to their school." She paused. "I didn't like making that call, but I had to do it. And if I had told you, I could have spared you an argument with your mother."

"I never thought of it that way, Pat. I guess I still have a lot to learn."

"You're doing fine," Pat said. "And now let me get to the reason why I dropped by. Aline, I have a favor to ask and I promise I'll understand if you say no. A lot of the girls who were on the lacrosse team this spring with Kerry graduated and have left for college. But last year's juniors, who are seniors now, are still coping with what happened to her. I believe it would be very helpful if they had a chance to share with you their feelings about Kerry. I'd like you to be the guidance counselor for these girls. Now, I understand if —"

Aline cut her off. "Pat, it's okay. It will be therapeutic for me too to hear about Kerry through the eyes of her friends. I'd love to work with them."

Pat left the office, promising to email the names. Aline experienced a tremendous sense of relief. She didn't have to invent a reason to spend time alone with these girls. Pat had given her one.

Before the first-period bell rang, she stopped into the teachers' lounge for a second cup of coffee. Several teachers were there, including Scott Kimball, who was talking to a very attractive history teacher who was new to the area. She was looking at him admiringly. I have to admit, Aline thought, he is a good-looking man. She guessed the new teacher, Barbara Bagli, to be about thirty, and that she was very interested in Scott.

Her suspicions were confirmed when Barbara told Scott, "My parents are going to be visiting next week from Cleveland, and they love to go out to nice restaurants. Where would you recommend?"

Waving Aline over to join them, he said, "Aline and I had a great dinner at the French restaurant La Petite in Nyack, last week. Aline, wasn't it terrific?"

Aline had assumed, incorrectly, that Scott would be discreet about their having spent an evening together. She looked around to see if any of the other teachers were privy to their conversation. She didn't think so. She tried to conceal her irritation as she answered, "La Petite is wonderful. I'm sure you and your parents will enjoy it, Barbara."

Aline walked over to the coffee machine to avoid further small talk. As she poured a cup for herself, she thought, That is the last time I will socialize with Scott Kimball outside of school and give him the chance to embarrass me.

43

Alan lived through the next week in a daze. He remembered unpacking his suitcase, hanging up some clothes and putting the rest in the dresser. Mom made sure I was neat, he thought. She'd give me a smack if I left clothes on the floor.

He didn't know what to do with himself. His father suggested that he try to find a temporary job. Temporary? he asked himself. How long is that? Until I go to trial and get convicted of murder?

Kerry's face was always in his mind. The fun things they had done together kept jumping back into his memory. The senior prom last May. The ride down to the shore afterward. Even though it was very late, they both got up early and took a walk on the beach. Again he could feel the warmth of the sand under his bare feet and hear Kerry's voice. "Alan, you were the best-looking guy at the prom. I'm so happy you let me pick your tux. It was perfect."

"And I was also the luckiest guy at the prom because I was with the most beautiful girl in the room."

Every day after breakfast he had driven to visit her grave. He stopped after noticing someone taking his picture next to the Dowling monument. The next day it had appeared on the front page of *The Record* newspaper.

Before he was arrested, he had always had a good appetite. Now it felt as if anything he ate stuck in his throat. His mother's constant reminders to eat made him feel even more stressed. Finally he burst out, "Mom, are you trying to fatten me up for my trial to show what good care you're taking of me?"

"Alan, these outbursts of yours are the kind of thing you pulled when you were a child. I didn't tolerate them then, and I'm not going to tolerate it now. I can understand that you are upset, but so are your father and I. We're not taking our anxiety out on you; don't take yours out on us."

Right to the end, Alan thought, Mom will run her tight ship.

As usual, she had the last word. "And don't forget. The only reason you are in this situation is because of your temper. If you hadn't quarreled with Kerry and had just told the truth, you'd be at Princeton right now."

After that exchange Alan vowed to say as little as possible to either of his parents. Unable to sleep at night, he slept most of the day.

His mother went back to her job as a critical care nurse at Englewood Hospital. His father had only taken two days off at the time of his arrest. He was back to catching the 7:14 A.M. train to the city.

The only one whose company he looked forward to was Brenda, their longtime housekeeper. Her sympathy and concern for him was a welcome change from his parents. One afternoon, after fixing him some pancakes, Brenda said, "Alan, I know there's no way in the world you hurt that poor girl. Everything is going to be okay for you. I can feel it in my bones, and my bones never lie."

A ghost of a smile came over Alan's face. "Take care of those bones, Brenda. They're the only things that believe in me."

By now all of his friends had left for their colleges. He had not heard from any of them. The several texts and emails he sent received no response. He could understand why Rich, Stan and Bobby were angry at him. But why had his other friends dropped him? Did he really have to ask?

The sense of isolation was suffocating. His father was right when he said he should try to get a job. But on a job application they ask if you have ever been arrested. How should I answer? "Yes, I'm charged with murder, and I'm wearing an ankle bracelet. But don't worry. I didn't do it."

After sleeping a good part of the day, Alan began to take long walks at night. He would drive to a walking trail, and carrying only a flashlight, he would take comfort in the solitude and quiet of the woods.

44

Seven players from last year's lacrosse team were still students at the high school. Thanks to Pat Tarleton's administrative assistance, Aline's counseling appointments with each of them were spaced far enough apart that no one had any suspicion about why she had been assigned to Aline.

With each session she began by saying, "I know you played lacrosse with my sister Kerry. I wonder if you would like to talk about how you felt about her and how you're feeling now."

As she expected, there was a pattern to the answers.

"I miss Kerry so much."

"I can't believe that anyone would deliberately hurt her."

"The party was so much fun, but then Kerry and Alan had the fight."

"Did the fight spoil the party?"

"Oh, no. Kerry, as usual, just laughed it

off. But I know they were texting back and forth after he left."

"Does anyone think that she should have broken up with him?"

"Only Annie. But you know why? She had a big crush on Alan."

When she broached the subject of who had brought the beer to the party, their answers were for the most part the same. "Some of the guys brought it. Kerry had some there."

Only one girl, Alexis, when asked about the beer, hesitated for a long minute before she said, "I have no idea."

Aline was sure she was holding back, but did not press her. She asked the girls if they had been with Kerry the day of the party. Four of them had been swimming in the pool with her from noon until three o'clock.

"Was anyone else there?" Aline asked.

Alexis said, "When Jamie Chapman came home from work, he yelled over to Kerry to ask if he could come swimming too."

"What did Kerry say?"

"Kerry liked Jamie. She told him to come over. Then he heard us talking about who was coming to the party. He asked Kerry if he could come. She told him it was only for kids who were still at the high school."

"How did he respond to that?"

He looked really disappointed. And when he left, Kerry said, "I feel bad turning him down, but we're having drinks at the party. He might talk about that to other people."

Aline decided to be candid with her next question. "The police believe that the guy who got Kerry the beer for her party had an argument with her. He's the one who recently helped her change a flat tire. They want to find that guy and talk to him. Did Kerry ever mention him to you?"

The only one who knew about the flat tire was Sinead Gilmartin. "Kerry told me she had a flat on Route 17 and she wasn't going to tell her father because he'd been after her to replace a bald tire."

"Do you know how long before the party that happened?"

"I guess about a week, maybe a little more."

"Sinead, do you recall anything Kerry told you that might help the police find this guy. What he looked like? The kind of car he was driving?"

"I think I remember. The guy who pulled over, Kerry said, was driving a tow truck. That's why he was able to change it so fast. She tried to give him a ten-dollar tip, but he turned it down. She said he was really nice."

It was information Mike would want to know immediately. As soon as Sinead left her office, Aline started typing an email to him, but then stopped. Don't send this through the school computer system, she thought. She took out her phone and sent Mike a text.

When Mike read the text from Aline, he seized on the words "tow truck." Although the information was still very general, it gave them more to work with than just some guy who was "about twenty-five" had stopped to help Kerry.

From his time on the Waldwick police force, he knew how most Traffic Safety units in Bergen County regulated their highways and roads. They had township Traffic Safety units that oversaw crossing guards and traffic lights. These units also maintained the list of tow truck operators who had a permit to work in their town. Waldwick, he recalled, had about a dozen companies with permits. He assumed Saddle River and the neighboring towns — Washington Township, Upper Saddle River, Woodcliff Lake, Ho-Ho-Kus — had a similar number.

There was no guarantee, however, that the tow truck he was interested in was on the permit list in a local town. Route 17 was a major highway serving northern New Jersey. Going five miles up or down the highway from Saddle River would bring in more towns and dozens more companies. But they had to start somewhere.

Mike assigned Sam Hines, a young investigator in his office, the task of tracking down each town's roster of companies with tow truck permits and contacting the companies to ask about their drivers who were under thirty years old.

"Mike, this is going to take a really long time," Sam said.

"I know. That's why I suggest you begin immediately."

45

The last student Pat Tarleton had suggested Aline work with was Valerie Long. Because she was a junior, the discussion of college choices could wait.

It was one of the economics teachers who brought matters to a head by stopping by Aline's office and telling her that Valerie was totally indifferent in class and seemed to be almost in a trance.

"Maybe if you talk to her, you can find out what the problem is," the teacher said.

The next day Aline scheduled a meeting with Valerie. When the girl came into her office, the sad expression on her face and in her eyes was clearly visible. Aline wondered if grief over Kerry's death might be the cause of her malaise.

She decided to go directly to that subject. After Valerie took a chair opposite hers, Aline said, "Valerie, I know many of the girls are very upset by Kerry's death, and I hear that you were very close to her."

"I loved Kerry. She was my best friend in school."

"Then I can understand why you feel so bad about her death."

"No, you can't."

Aline paused, hoping Valerie would say more. But when she didn't, Aline knew that there was no point in pressing her. Instead she said, "Valerie, I reviewed your records. Your marks at your former school were very good. They were strong after you arrived here last January. But then they fell off considerably. And this year your teachers are concerned that you seem distracted in class."

I am distracted, Valerie thought, but I can't tell why. Instead she said, "I miss my friends in Chicago. They're all there. My stepfather changed jobs, and overnight they told me we were moving. I wanted to live with my grandmother in Chicago and stay in my former school, but they wouldn't let me."

"What about your biological father?" Aline asked.

Valerie smiled spontaneously. "He was wonderful. I was Daddy's little girl. He found out he had brain cancer and was dead in two months."

"How old were you when that happened?"

"He died on my eighth birthday."

"I'm so sorry. I'm sure that was very difficult for you."

"Whatever. My mother knows better than to have a celebration on my birthday. She remarried two years ago. Wayne," she said derisively, "is twenty years older than my mother."

There are multiple reasons Valerie is floundering, Aline thought. She misses her Chicago friends. She lost Kerry, her only friend here. She's still grieving for her natural father, and she resents her stepfather.

Aline decided that the next thing to do was to arrange a meeting with both of Valerie's parents and discuss with them Valerie's obvious resentment about the move. And if that might be a factor in her lack of interest in her schoolwork.

"Valerie," she said, "as you know, Kerry was my sister. I of all people can understand how sad you are to lose her. It's hard to make friends in a new environment, especially when all the other students have known each other for a long time. I can only imagine how difficult it was for you to lose your best friend."

"You have *no idea* how difficult it was,"

Valerie said.

"Valerie, I know that Kerry would want you to make new friends and keep up with your schoolwork."

"I'll try," Valerie said indifferently.

Then as she looked into Aline's face and saw the sadness in her eyes, she wondered if someday she could tell Aline what was really going on.

46

June Crowley went to Mass every Sunday, but she was a practicing Catholic in the loosest definition of the phrase. It was just as important to her to be beautifully dressed as it was to attend the sacraments. Over the years it had never occurred to her to have a private conversation with Father Frank. But now, because she was frantic with worry about Alan, she decided to have a talk with him.

She called and asked if she could meet with him as soon as possible. He suggested that the next morning would be a good time for him.

When she arrived at his office, she was still framing in her mind how to tell him about her concerns. But when she was there, she simply blurted out the words.

"Father, I'm desperately worried that Alan may be suicidal."

Father Frank was well aware that Alan

Crowley had been arrested. He had been thinking of calling June and Doug to tell them how sorry he was for both them and Alan. Now he was deeply concerned that June might be right.

"What makes you think that, June?" he asked.

"It's the way he's acting. He sleeps most of the day and then takes off right after dinner. I don't know where he goes, or if he's even talking to anyone. And I doubt that. He swears that he was not the one who hurt Kerry, but he knows that everyone believes he did it and everybody expects that when he goes on trial, he'll be found guilty and sent to prison for many years."

"June, you're a nurse, do you know any psychiatrists who could talk to him?"

"I've suggested that to him. He flat out refuses to go."

"Do you think it would help if I had a talk with him?"

"It would be a great relief to me if you did."

"It will be better if I can catch him alone. Are you and Doug working tomorrow afternoon?"

"Yes, we are."

"Okay, I'll drop by in the late afternoon and see if I can get him to speak to me."

"Our housekeeper Brenda will be there. I'll tell her to let you in."

The next afternoon Father Frank drove to the Crowley home and rang the bell. It was answered immediately by a middle-aged woman he assumed was the housekeeper.

"You must be Brenda," he said. "I'm Father Frank."

"Mrs. Crowley told me you would be stopping by," Brenda replied.

"Is Alan home?"

"Yes, he's in the den watching TV. Should I tell him you're here?"

"No, just show me the den, and I'll take it from there."

"Can I get you anything to drink?"

"No, thank you. I'm fine."

As Father Frank stood at the door of the TV room, Brenda made a noisy retreat in the direction of the kitchen.

Alan was watching a movie. He didn't look up when the priest opened the door and walked into the room.

Father Frank barely recognized Alan, whose appearance was quite different from the well-groomed young man he often saw in church. He was wearing an old T-shirt that looked like he had slept in it and gym shorts. A pair of scuffed sneakers was next to him on the floor. It was obvious he hadn't shaved in several days. It looked as though he hadn't bothered to comb his hair.

Alan looked up. A surprised expression came over his face. "I didn't know you were coming, Father Frank."

"Your mother is very concerned about you. She believes that you're depressed."

"Wouldn't you feel depressed if you were facing a long prison term?"

"Yes, I would, Alan."

"Well, Father, don't be disappointed. If you came over to hear my confession, I'm sorry to say I didn't do it."

"Alan, I came over to talk to you and to hear what you had to say."

"Then let me say it clearly. I loved Kerry. I still love her. That night I went over to help her clean up. She told me she was tired. We could do it in the morning. I kissed her good night and went home. I know I lied about that to the police and asked the guys to lie for me. But you know why I did that? I was scared. Wouldn't you be scared if suddenly everybody was looking at you like you're a killer? Do you know what it's like to have handcuffs on and be forced to wear an orange jumpsuit?"

"So you're telling me that you are innocent of Kerry's death."

"I'm not just telling you; I'm swearing it

to you. If you have a Bible with you, I'll swear on that. But it's obvious nobody believes me."

"Alan, in my experience, the truth has a way of coming out. If you do go to trial, I'm sure that will be many months from now. What are you going to do between now and then?"

"Frankly, Father, I've been spending a lot of time thinking how nice it would be to be with Kerry again."

"Alan, you're not thinking of hurting yourself, are you? Think of what that would do to your mother and father."

"It would be easier for them if I just wasn't around, rather than watch me get convicted in court."

Deeply concerned, Father Frank said, "Let me remind you that it will probably be a year or more before you go to trial. By that time your situation may have changed."

"Wouldn't that be nice," Alan said matter-of-factly.

When Father Frank left, he was deeply disturbed remembering what Marge had told him about Jamie being in the pool and how fearful she was that if the police found that out, they might get him to tell them that he was the one who had hit Kerry.

What should I do? What *can* I do?

214

He did not know that Brenda had been in the hallway catching every word and that she couldn't wait to tell Marge all about it.

47

Brenda could barely stay near the speed limit as she drove over to Marge's house. She had called Marge to confirm she was home and that it would be okay to come over. It was obvious that Marge had seen her coming up the driveway, because the door had been left open.

Breathlessly, she recounted how Father Frank had dropped in to see Alan. "He came over because June and Doug Crowley are afraid he is suicidal."

"Oh, dear God!" Marge exclaimed.

"That poor boy! No wonder they're worried. He's convinced that he's going to prison for killing Kerry Dowling. He swore on the Bible that he is innocent."

"What did Father Frank say to Alan?" Marge asked anxiously.

"He was pleading with him to have faith. He told him he won't go to trial for at least a year, and a lot can happen in that time. I just pray that he convinced Alan that he shouldn't harm himself."

"I pray that too," Marge said with a tremor in her voice.

Having delivered the day's gossip, Brenda looked at her watch. "Gotta go," she said. "I have to shop for dinner."

Marge sat trembling at the thought that Alan would commit suicide. She distracted herself from that thought by turning on the five o'clock news. Just as she returned to her chair, Jamie came into the room.

The newscast began and Alan's picture appeared on the screen. "That's Alan Crowley, Mom," he said excitedly.

"Yes, I know it is, Jamie."

The reporter was speaking while footage of Alan at the courthouse was shown in the background. "Rumors are swirling that Lester Parker, attorney for accused killer Alan Crowley, has approached the Bergen County Prosecutor about a plea bargain. We contacted Lester Parker and he adamantly denied that rumor."

"Why is Alan on TV?" Jamie asked his mother.

"The police think he hurt Kerry the night she died in her pool."

"He went home."

"I know, Jamie. They think he hurt Kerry

and then went home."

"No. Alan Crowley gave Kerry a hug and a kiss and then he went home. The Big Guy hurt Kerry."

Aghast, Marge stared at him. "Jamie, are you sure Alan didn't hurt Kerry and push her in the pool?"

"No, the Big Guy did. Alan went home. I'm hungry. What's for dinner?"

48

Aline was worried about Valerie Long. Something was not quite right about the girl, and it was more than just the loss of Kerry's friendship. The word that came to Aline's mind was "despairing." In a meeting with Pat Tarleton, Aline shared with her how concerned she was about Valerie after their talk.

"I think you should speak to the parents and get their version of what is going on," Pat told her.

"I agree, but I have a feeling Valerie would be very unhappy if she knew I was planning to meet with her mother and stepfather. Do you think I should arrange to see them someplace outside of school?"

"No, I don't. It's against our school's policy to have this type of meeting away from our building. It's the parents' decision to tell or not tell Valerie that they're coming in to talk to you. If she finds out they were here, they're on their own to come up with an explanation as to why."

Glad to have Pat's approval, Aline looked up the contact information for Valerie's parents. She decided to start with the mother and dialed her cell phone number. It was answered on the first ring.

The screen on Marina Long's phone showed that the call was from Saddle River High School. Her first words were "Is Valerie all right?" The question made it easer for Aline to go directly to the reason for the call.

"Mrs. Long, everything is okay. Valerie is in class. My name is Aline Dowling. I'm Valerie's guidance counselor at school. But I have some concerns about Valerie that I want to talk to you and your husband about."

"Aline, I'm glad you called. We have concerns too, and we're not sure what to do. Wayne and I would welcome the opportunity to meet with you."

It was agreed that the Longs would meet Aline the next day.

Later that day Aline heard a knock on her office door. When she called, "Come in," she was surprised to see Scott Kimball enter and settle into the chair opposite her. Her first thought was that she had not invited him to sit.

"Aline," he began, "I know you're annoyed at me, and you have a right to be. That was a big faux pas on my part the other day in the teachers' lounge. You had made it clear that there was to be no talk of our having socialized off school property. As the saying goes, 'loose lips sink ships.' I'm here to apologize."

Aline wasn't sure what to say. She had rehearsed a speech where she was going to blast him for talking about their dinner in front of another teacher. Now he had apologized and seemed genuinely contrite.

"Okay, Scott. We all make mistakes. Let's let it go."

"Thanks Aline. I really appreciate that."

He hesitated. "Aline, I want to ask you to do something with me. It would be strictly on a professional basis. Tomorrow night at seven there is a seminar at Montclair State about the stresses faced by high school student athletes. As a teacher and a coach, I'm obviously interested, and I'm planning to go. I assume this type of presentation would be of interest to you as a guidance counselor. Would you like to go?"

Aline started to answer, but Scott kept talking.

"Just so you know, we'll be doing this as two professionals. I know better than to ask if you want to ride over with me. You don't even have to sit with me when we're there. But I warn you. I'm going to be hungry when it ends at eight-thirty. There's an excellent chance I'm going to ask you to join me for dinner. As professionals, of course."

Aline found herself smiling. Scott was a charmer. Three minutes ago he had been one hundred percent in her doghouse. Now she found herself looking forward to spending time with him tomorrow night.

"All right, Mr. Kimball," she said, "I'll meet you at the seminar. Regarding dinner afterwards, let's see what tomorrow brings."

49

After a sleepless night, Marge knew that she had to talk to Father Frank again. As soon as Jamie left to walk to Acme, she called him. He said, "Marge, come to my office right now. I've been thinking a lot about our last discussion."

Marge had not expected to be invited in so quickly. She had wanted time to plan what she would say to Father Frank about what Jamie had told her. Now she only had the ten-minute car ride to the rectory to organize her thoughts.

The priest answered the door himself and escorted Marge to his office. They sat in two chairs facing each other.

"Father, when Jamie and I were in the kitchen last night, Alan Crowley's picture came on the television. When I told Jamie why Alan was on TV, Jamie started talking again about what he saw the night of Kerry's party."

She hesitated.

Father Frank said, "Marge, I can see you're upset. But I think it will help if you just tell me what is worrying you."

"I know you understand that Jamie's memory can be hazy. He mixes together things that didn't happen at the same time."

"I know that, Marge," Father Frank said sympathetically.

"Last night, Jamie was very specific when he described what he saw happened to Kerry."

"What did he say?"

"When I explained to him that the police think Alan is the one who hurt Kerry, Jamie was sure that Alan didn't do it."

Father Frank leaned forward in his chair. "Marge, what exactly did Jamie say?"

"He told me that Alan hugged and kissed Kerry, and then he went home. Then somebody else, 'the Big Guy,' hurt Kerry and pushed her in the pool."

"Marge, do you think Jamie is describing what he saw accurately?"

"Yes, I do. But I don't know what to do."

Tears began running down Marge's cheeks. She reached over and began to fumble in her pocketbook. "Father, is there someplace I could get a glass of water?"

"I'm sorry, Marge," Father Frank said as

he headed toward the kitchen. "I should have offered earlier." When he returned with the water, he noticed how pale she looked. "Are you okay?"

Marge reached for the water glass, took a sip and swallowed a pill. "Honestly, Father, I'm having some problems with my heart. When I'm feeling stressed, like I am right now, I have to take one of these. It's a nitroglycerine pill."

Father Frank waited while she took a few more sips of water. "These pills are miraculous," she said. "I feel better already."

Marge continued. "About Jamie, if what he told me is true, Alan Crowley is innocent. But how do I let Jamie talk to the police and risk having the police think Jamie hurt Kerry? I told you how Jack would call Jamie the Big Guy. If Jamie tells the police 'the Big Guy' hurt Kerry, they might think he's talking about himself. Father, I want to help Alan Crowley, but I can't do it if it means getting Jamie in trouble."

"Marge, I don't believe for a minute that Jamie was the one who hurt Kerry. I know you don't either. Wouldn't it be best to tell the police what Jamie said, and just have faith in the system to work?"

"I don't know, Father. I just need more time to think about it."

50

Aline was about to leave her office when her cell phone rang. It was Mike Wilson.

"Aline," he asked, "could you possibly meet me tonight? There are some things I want to go over with you."

"Of course."

"O'Malley's at seven o'clock?"

"Fine. I'll see you there."

When she arrived at O'Malley's, Mike was waiting for her. He was seated at the same table in the corner they had chosen the last time.

"It appears that you are a creature of habit," Aline said.

"Guilty as charged," Mike replied.

"My, aren't we formal?" Aline said, noting how handsome Mike looked in his jacket and tie.

"Whenever I testify in court, I wear my Sunday best. I spent this afternoon getting grilled by a defense attorney."

"Who won?" Aline asked.

"If they don't find this defendant guilty, there is no justice in the world."

The waiter approached the table. Mike asked, "Are we both creatures of habit?"

Aline nodded.

"A Pinot Grigio for the lady, and I'll have a Coors Light.

"So, Aline, how is the world of guidance?"

"Sometimes easy, and sometimes not. I've got a depressed student I'm really worried about. Her parents are coming in to meet with me tomorrow. Oh! I have a potential update on Alan Crowley."

"Really?"

"Princeton is aware of the accusations against Alan. My understanding is that in cases like these, they insist that the student stay home." She decided against sharing with him that her mother and Pat Tarleton had contacted Princeton.

"I'm not surprised," Mike said. "Colleges have media tracking services. They would have picked up reports that 'Princeton-bound Alan Crowley' has been accused of a crime."

Mike took a long sip of his beer and then asked, "How are your parents doing?"

"I guess as well as can be expected. My mother is so sure that Alan is guilty. I think it's given her some peace that he's been arrested."

"The families of victims often react that way. They consider it the first step toward justice. It might be a good idea for your mother to join a victim's support group. I've seen people who were helped a lot. I'll send you some information on the groups."

"Thanks. I appreciate that."

"Aline, let me get to the main reason I asked you to meet me tonight. As I've told you, a weakness in our case against Alan is that we haven't found the tire changer who had the incident with Kerry. The information you sent me that he was a tow truck driver is very helpful. In your text you said one of the girls who appears to know something may be holding back. It's so important that we find this guy and confirm where he was the night of the party. Can you find a reason to spend more time with that girl and maybe get her to say more?"

Aline sighed. "I may be en route to a very short career as a guidance counselor if they find out what I've been doing."

"Aline, I don't have to know the girl's name. I just need the information. And I promise you, nobody will know the information came from you."

In her mind Aline relived Alexis Jaccarino's distinct hesitation when she asked her about the guy who changed Kerry's tire.

"I'll figure out a reason to have that girl come to my office and get her talking."

It was on the tip of Mike's tongue to ask Aline to stay and have dinner with him again. But if a defense attorney thought that a detective and a witness on a case were dating, he would rip both of them to shreds on cross-examination.

Ten minutes later Mike had finished his beer and Aline her wine. He signaled for the check. "Back to the office for me. I'm on the witness stand again tomorrow morning. I have to go over my reports."

"And I can catch the end of dinner with my parents. I try to be around them as much as possible, and I have plans for tomorrow night."

They walked to their cars. Mike was disappointed that he couldn't ask Aline to dinner.

She was disappointed that he didn't.

51

Aline's call to Valerie's mother only heightened the feelings of concern she and Wayne had about Valerie. Marina was relieved when Wayne quickly agreed to work from home so that he could go with her to the high school. Hoping to avoid being seen by Valerie, they arrived at Aline's office promptly at 11:00.

The mother, whose resemblance to Valerie was striking, looked to be in her late thirties. The stepfather had a head full of steel-gray hair and appeared to be in his mid- to late fifties. Aline's initial impression was that he reminded her of the actor Richard Gere.

After introductions were completed, Marina Long asked, "Why are you worried about Valerie?"

Her direct question required a direct answer. "I saw in her records that she did well at her previous high school in Chicago. But since coming here, her marks have gone down considerably. And she seems depressed," Aline told them.

Marina nodded. "We know. And we've been so worried about her." Marina was obviously on the verge of tears.

Aline watched as Wayne put his hand over his wife's hand. He said, "I know I'm the major cause of the problem. From the first time she met me, she didn't like me. She thought I was trying to replace her father. I wasn't. Every effort I made to build a relationship with her was rejected. I have two sons who live in California. I'm a widower. My first wife and I always hoped we would have a daughter as well."

Marina added, "Valerie tries to give people the impression that he ignores his sons. The fact is Wayne often travels to San Francisco. He always sees them when he's there. It was harder for them to come to Chicago because they both have young families. And last year when Wayne and I went out to see them for Thanksgiving, Valerie insisted on staying home to be with her grandmother."

"Did Valerie tell you why we moved from Chicago?" Wayne asked.

"Yes. She said you were offered a better job with a bigger salary and you took it. That resulted in her being apart from her Chicago friends."

"That's not what happened," Wayne said, the frustration clear in his voice. "I am a branch manager for Merrill Lynch. The branch office I ran was shut in a consolidation. I was offered a better position in Manhattan and I had to give them an answer right away." Looking at his wife, he said, "We agreed I should accept it."

Aline said, "One of the things that puzzles me is that when Valerie came to Saddle River last January, at least marks wise she got off to a good start. But something changed in the spring. Do you have any idea what that might have been?"

Marina said, "Last May her paternal grandmother had a stroke and passed away. Valerie had stayed very close to her after her father died."

"For a young person, she has experienced a great deal of loss," Aline said. "Have you considered having her see a psychiatrist?"

"Of course, we have," Marina said. "Twice I tried to introduce the idea. Both times she got furious and upset. We decided it would do more harm than good to keep bringing that up."

"As you probably know," Aline said, "my sister Kerry died two weeks ago."

Wayne interrupted. "We know, and we're

terribly sorry. We read about it in the papers."

"Valerie told me that she considered Kerry to be her closest friend at this school. Did she ever tell you that?"

"No," Marina said. "I know how shocked she was when Kerry died, but I thought she knew Kerry more as a teammate than a friend."

"Apparently they were close. That makes yet another loss in your daughter's life."

"Then where do we go from here?" Wayne asked.

"I'm going to keep in close touch with Valerie and her teachers. I'll monitor her progress and will keep both of you informed. Of course, if you notice any changes, let me know."

As the Longs left the office, Aline was more concerned than ever about Valerie.

52

Father Frank knew that he must try to persuade Marge to share with the police what Jamie had told her. He understood Marge's horror that the police might focus on Jamie as the killer. But it was not fair to have Alan on the verge of suicide when there was a witness who could exonerate him.

Father Frank had replayed the two conversations with Marge a dozen times in his mind. She had *confided* in him, which is very different from being in the state of sacrament. If she had asked him to hear her confession, his obligation to remain silent would have been absolute. But since she had merely confided in him, the sacrament of penance did not apply. If Marge would not do so, it was his obligation to share what he knew with the police.

After her conversation with Father Frank, Marge's conscience continued to weigh heavily on her. She had asked Jamie twice over the past two days to repeat what he saw happen in Kerry's yard before he went swimming with her. Both times he told the same story. "Alan kissed Kerry goodbye. Then he went home. Then the Big Guy hit Kerry and pushed her into the pool." He added, "Daddy called me 'the Big Guy.' He's in Heaven with Kerry."

The idea that Alan was going through a living hell for something he didn't do gnawed at Marge. That was why when she called Father Frank and he said he could come over, it was a relief. She had decided to discuss with him how to go about contacting the police.

The doorbell rang at three-thirty. Jamie had gone straight from work to watch the school teams practice. Marge was relieved that he would not be home when she spoke to Father Frank.

When she answered the bell, Father Frank followed her into the modest living room, which was scrupulously neat. She invited him to sit down and pointed at a large overstuffed chair that reminded him of the furniture in his grandmother's house.

"That was Jack's favorite chair," Marge said. "After his grandmother died, Jack brought it home."

"It's very comfortable, Marge."

"I'm sorry, Father. I'm talking about furniture because I'm too nervous to talk about the reason I asked you to come over."

"Marge, I was planning to call you. I think I know what you want to talk about."

"It's not right for me to keep quiet while Alan Crowley is in so much trouble."

Father Frank remained silent to allow her to continue.

Marge bit her lip. "Since I spoke to you, I have asked Jamie twice to tell me what he saw the night of Kerry's party. Both times he repeated that Alan kissed Kerry and then went home." She looked away as though gathering strength. "I know in my heart of hearts Jamie never would have hurt Kerry. I have to tell the police what I know."

"Marge, you are making the right decision." Father Frank tried to conceal the relief he felt that Marge had reached that conclusion on her own.

"Father, I don't have any money. Obviously, neither does Jamie. I understand there are lawyers that will help people like us for free."

"Do you mean public defenders?"

"Yes, if that's what they call them. I'd like to speak to one now, before I talk to the police about Jamie."

"Marge, from what I understand, it doesn't work that way. They will make a public defender available to someone who has been accused of something. I don't think they can help you before then."

"I have ten thousand dollars in my savings account. Will that be enough for a lawyer?"

"Marge, I don't know a lot about how much lawyers charge. I do know that one of our parishioners, Greg Barber, is a very good attorney. For much less than his usual fee, he has worked with our parishioners who needed his help. If you would like, I'll reach out to him for you."

"I would appreciate it so much."

"I'll speak to him this evening. I know he'll want to help you."

That evening Father Frank phoned Greg's home. Greg's wife told him he was finishing a case in Atlanta and would return in four days. She gave Father Frank his cell phone number. Father Frank immediately called Greg, who promised that he would try to help Marge and asked that she call his office the day he got back.

Father Frank called Marge and told her about the lawyer's schedule. They both agreed that she should wait to speak to him before contacting the police. He would remain in touch with Alan Crowley to make sure he was all right. Hopefully, a few more days would not make any difference.

53

The seminar, as promised, concluded promptly at 8:30. Aline was happy she had decided to go. The presenters had offered interesting insights about how some student athletes turn sports, which should be a stress reliever, into an additional source of stress. The problem was often made worse by parents and coaches who focus solely on winning.

The small auditorium appeared to be about half-filled. As she was standing up to leave, Aline looked around. She was relieved when she did not recognize anyone she knew.

As they started to walk outside, Scott said, "Now for the $64,000 question." His hands pretended to do a drumroll. "I know a wonderful Italian restaurant nearby. And I promise I won't practice my fractured French on you."

"I enjoyed brushing up on my French."

She followed him to a restaurant that was less than a mile away and pulled up next to him in the parking lot. When she got out of her car, he was holding up a wine carrier with two bottles. "It's a bring-your-own restaurant. I brought a Chardonnay and a Pinot Noir, just in case you said yes."

Once inside, Scott ordered from the menu in surprisingly good Italian.

"You didn't tell me you know Italian as well."

"My grandmother was from Italy. She loved to talk to me in Italian. Fortunately, I remember most of it."

"You are a man of many hidden talents," Aline said, smiling.

"My mother would often say that to me. And then my aunt would always chime in, 'If you're so damn smart, why ain't you *rich*?' "

The calamari and the veal were excellent. Their conversation glided easily from politics to favorite movies. When they were finishing their cappuccinos, Aline brought up a topic that had been in the back of her mind all evening.

"Scott, I've been meaning to ask you about a student I'm really concerned about. I'm sure you know her because she played varsity lacrosse."

"Who are you worried about?"

"Valerie Long, the girl who transferred to Saddle River last January. I met with her parents today."

"It sounds serious. What's wrong?"

"She appears to be withdrawn and depressed. One of her teachers has already spoken to me about her appearing distracted."

"I'm so sorry to hear this."

"The reason I bring it up is, as her coach, you got to work closely with Valerie last spring. Is she in any of your math classes?"

"No, not this year."

"What was your impression of her when you coached her?"

"Frankly, she's a kid with two personalities. On the sidelines she is shy, often standing someplace off by herself. Put her in the game and she goes into attack mode. She's the most aggressive player on the field.

"But when the game's over, it's back to quiet and timid. She was the only sophomore on the varsity squad. I know Kerry tried particularly hard to make her feel included."

"Was Valerie close to any of the other girls?"

"Not really. I tried to be, what's the word, *available* to her. But she kept me at a distance as well."

"Do you see her often in school now?"

"Lacrosse isn't until the spring, so I don't see her every day like I used to. We'll pass in the hallway and say hi to each other. Nothing really beyond that."

"Okay. I'm just trying to figure out a way to get through to her."

"I'll try to help, engage her in conversation. Maybe she'll open up to one of us."

"Thanks. And thank you again for dinner."

54

As Nancy Carter glanced out her kitchen window, she found it hard to believe how quickly the last two weeks had flown by. She and her husband Carl had agreed that he would take their son Tony to Alaska on a fishing trip. It would be a break in every sense of the word. Workaholic Carl would see that his partners at his civil engineering firm were perfectly capable of running the business while he was away. Tony would break his habit of constantly being on social media by leaving his cell phone home. Carl had brought his phone, with the understanding that Nancy would contact them only in the event of a dire emergency.

And, she admitted to herself, although she dearly loved her husband, it was a nice break for her.

But in the two weeks they were away, Nancy wondered if she should have let Tony know that Kerry Dowling had been murdered.

Tony had gone to Saddle River High School for two years and was about to start at Choate, the famous boarding school in Connecticut, where he would do his junior and senior year. He and Kerry had known each other from the time they had been in student government together. Nancy knew he would be very sad to hear of her death and learn that he had missed her wake and funeral. That was precisely why she had decided not to tell him about what happened to her while he was away.

She had checked the United Airline app. Their flight had landed in Newark on time. The sound of car doors opening and closing in the driveway announced their arrival.

After hugs all around and carrying in their gear, they sat at the kitchen table.

Carl introduced the conversation Nancy had been so concerned about. "So, did we miss anything while we were away?"

Looking at Tony, she said, "I'm sorry to say yes. Something terrible happened while you were away." She told them about Kerry's tragic death and the police investigation.

Tony immediately grabbed his cell phone off the charger and reviewed the messages his friends had sent him about Kerry. They repeated the same information. Kerry had a party on Saturday night. Her father and sister found her dead in the pool around noon on Sunday. Kerry and Alan had a fight at the party.

"We were away for two weeks," Carl said. "When did this happen?"

"I heard about it on the radio literally while you were on your way to the airport to start your trip. Then Alan was arrested. From what I've read in the papers and seen on the news, the police believe Alan went back after the party was over and killed Kerry."

"So Mom, they found her in the pool Sunday morning, around the time Dad and the limo picked me up at the Acme?" Tony asked.

"That's right, Tony, and I hope you'll understand why I didn't —"

Waving her off, Tony said, "No, Mom. That's okay. Did the papers say anything about Jamie Chapman?"

"Jamie Chapman?" Nancy said incredulously. "No, why would they?"

"That was the Sunday Dad and I left on the trip, right?"

"Yes," Nancy answered. "Dad left here in the limo and picked you up at Acme, and you went straight to the airport."

What he was trying to remember came back to Tony. "I noticed Jamie's sneakers," he said. Then he blurted out, "He had new sneakers. He was showing them off to everyone. I know he was wearing them on Saturday because he asked me a bunch of times if I liked them. But he wasn't wearing them on that Sunday. The ones he had on were all scuffed up. I asked him why he changed them. He said they got wet because he was swimming in the pool with Kerry *after* her party."

His mother and father stared at him. *"After her party?"* they both said in unison.

"Are you sure that's what Jamie told you?" his father asked.

"Dad, I'm positive."

Walking over to the phone, Carl said, "Tony, you have to tell the police what you just told us." He began dialing the number of the Saddle River Police Department. They took Carl's name and phone number and said they would immediately notify Detective Wilson of his call.

55

Marina Long and her husband Wayne had been concerned about Valerie ever since they moved from Chicago to Saddle River. They understood that it had been an abrupt and dramatic change for her, but had hoped and expected that her new school, which was highly rated, would bring her around. At her previous school, even though she was innately shy, she'd had many close friends. They had now been in New Jersey for nine months. That should have been enough time to make new friends. But where are they? Marina asked herself. Valerie always seems to be alone.

Marina had taken the afternoon off. She had hoped to spend some time with her daughter. But when Valerie came home from school, she went straight to her room and closed the door behind her. When Marina called her for dinner shortly after Wayne got home, she was her usual distant self. They both tried to initiate a conversation by asking about the outlook for this year's lacrosse team. Her one-word answer was "Good." It was over coffee and Valerie's favorite apple pie dessert that Marina broached the subject with her.

"Valerie, Miss Dowling called and asked us to meet with her. We went over to the school this morning."

Valerie half-closed her eyes as though in denial. "She had no right to do that," she said fiercely.

"She had every right," Marina said. "Apparently, the teachers are worried about the way you are in class."

"What's wrong with the way I am in class?" Valerie asked defensively.

"You appear to be distracted, and your marks went downhill shortly after we moved here."

"They'll go back up," Valerie said.

"Is there any reason why your marks changed?" Wayne said gently.

When she did not answer, he said, "Look, Valerie. I think you have resented my presence since your mother and I got together. Let's see if we can clear the air right now.

"My first wife and I always hoped to have a daughter. Of course, that didn't happen, and Lucy died around the same time as your father. I know what it's like to lose someone you're very close to. When you lost your dad, you were heartbroken. I know I can't replace him, and I don't want to. But I want you to know that I want to be close to you. I consider you the daughter I never had."

Valerie looked away.

"Val, we know that the move was abrupt," Marina said, "and I told you that Wayne had gotten a big promotion. That was absolutely true. But the fact is that the Chicago office where he worked was being closed, and if he didn't accept the offer in New York he would have been out of work."

Valerie did not answer. Marina looked at her and said, "Valerie, your father loved you very much. I'm sure that it's a great comfort to Daddy to know that Wayne is here for you, and he loves you."

Valerie considered telling what was really happening, but her lips would not form the words. She had told Kerry, the only person she felt she could confide in, and Kerry was dead. She shook her head, as though dismissing what her mother and stepfather had told her. She pushed back her chair and abruptly left the table.

Marina followed her up the stairs.

"Valerie, something is upsetting you that

you won't talk about. But you can't live with it. You've lost Daddy and your grandmother. I think what you need to do is speak to a therapist, someone who can help you."

"Do me a favor, Mom. Leave me alone," Valerie said as she shut the door to her room.

56

As he drove to the Chapman home, Mike was still trying to process the ramifications of the meeting he had that morning with Tony Carter and his father. "Jamie Chapman said he went swimming with Kerry *after* her party." Tony was absolutely certain about his recollection of what Jamie had told him. The impact on the investigation could not be underestimated.

Mike had tried to impress on Tony and his parents that they should not share Tony's information about Jamie. But he was concerned. He got the impression that they were talkers.

Kerry's body had been discovered by her family at 11:15 A.M. that Sunday morning. The forensic report from the medical examiner could provide only a rough estimate of how long she had been in the water. Kerry had sent a text at 11:10 P.M. telling Alan not to come over to her house. Assuming she was the one who sent the text, and Mike had no reason to believe otherwise, that was the latest time he could document that she was alive.

Alan's three friends and the waitress at Nellie's confirmed that Alan left Nellie's at approximately 11:15. The 3.9-mile drive from Nellie's to the Dowling home would have taken Alan about eleven minutes. Was it possible that Jamie went swimming with Kerry *after* 11:00, when the party ended, but *before* Alan returned to the house? Very unlikely.

He had brought fellow detective Andy Nerlino with him because he wanted to question Marge and Jamie out of each other's presence. "I interviewed them the day the body was discovered," Mike told him. "My last thought when I left the house was that their answers sounded rehearsed."

"Understood."

When they reached the Chapman home, Mike rang the front doorbell. There was no answer. They walked around the house to see if the Chapmans were in the backyard. When they were not there, Andy walked over to the back door and knocked on it. Then he said, "Mike, come over here and take a look at this."

He was pointing at a small smudge stain

on the white wooden door, just below the handle.

"Blood?" Mike asked as he leaned in closer for a look.

"It might be." Andy said.

Mike took out his cell phone and snapped several pictures of the stain, then dialed his office. "I need an evidence tech right away," he said crisply.

Twenty minutes later the tech arrived. He removed a portion of the stain and placed it in an evidence bag.

Mike and Andy agreed that it was just as well the Chapmans weren't home. "We need to know if this stain is blood and whose it is before we talk to them," Mike said. "We'll ask for a rush at the lab, but even then it will take a few days to get the results. I'm going to call the Carters again and emphasize how absolutely important it is that they keep their mouths shut."

57

The police had insisted Tony Carter say nothing about his statement to them. For a few days he managed to comply. But when word got back to the Carters that someone reported seeing police cars at Marge Chapman's home, he couldn't help himself. His mother and father were no better at staying silent.

Tony's story — "I helped solve Kerry's murder; Alan Crowley is innocent; Jamie Chapman was the last one to be with Kerry when she was alive" — spread through the town like wildfire.

Instead of being elated, Alan's reaction surprised his parents. "The police have this all screwed up," he said matter-of-factly. "I saw Kerry and Jamie together lots of times. There's no way he killed her any more than I did."

"I can't believe you're not excited and thrilled," June snapped. "I think we should call Princeton right now."

"Mom, don't get too excited about the stuff on Jamie. I'm telling you they're wrong. When they figure that out, guess who they're going to come back to?" he said, while pointing at his chest.

Annoyed at her son's reaction to the stunning news, June stormed out of the room and went upstairs. Her tone of voice exultant, she called Lester Parker and told him about Tony Carter.

Parker said, "June, I was just going to call you. I have just heard the rumor that a neighbor might have been in the pool with Kerry after the party. But let's not go too fast on this one. My understanding is that the young man who claims he was in the pool with her has a substantial intellectual disability. The police might conclude that his story is a fantasy or a fabrication or just not something they can rely on."

When June hung up the phone, she felt deflated, but at the same time more optimistic. Despite Lester Parker's caution, Alan had to realize that the police were looking at another suspect. She was hoping this would lift his mood enough to keep at bay any more thoughts of harming himself.

58

It was lunchtime when several students came over to Aline and excitedly told her about Tony Carter going to the police. Her instinctive reaction was that Jamie would never hurt Kerry. She had started babysitting for him when he was eight years old. Kerry was six at the time. She would often bring Kerry along when she sat at Jamie's house or, in swimming weather, would bring Jamie to her house.

He was always so gentle in every way, she thought. He loved Kerry so much.

She went directly home after school. The front door was unlocked. "Mom," Aline called as she walked in.

"Out here" was her mother's response from the patio in back.

Fran was sitting on one of the lounge chairs near where Steve had laid down Kerry's lifeless body after he carried her out of the pool. Aline wondered how often her mother sat there and why she would have chosen that spot.

Fran's first words were "By now I assume you have heard about Tony Carter. I wonder how much the Crowleys paid the Carters to have Tony spread that story. It's disgusting that they would try to place the blame on someone like Jamie who can't even defend himself."

"Mom, why would the Carters do that?"

"I'll tell you why. It's because they're social climbers. I myself have heard June Crowley say that Carl Carter is always pestering Doug to sponsor him to join Ridgewood Country Club. What a trade-off to blame poor, innocent Jamie for a crime their son committed."

"Mom, you know how much I care about Jamie," Aline protested, "but I simply cannot believe that the Crowleys got Tony Carter to lie for them."

"You've been defending Alan from day one. I don't understand you."

"Mom, you tried and convicted Alan on day one. I don't understand you!"

"Then we agree to disagree," Fran said firmly.

"Look, Mom, the last thing I want to do is to have us getting upset with each other. And I can tell you this. Remember Mike

Wilson asked you and Dad about whether you knew about the flat tire Kerry had?"

"Yes, and she hadn't told us about it because Dad had been after her to pick up a new tire."

"The police still haven't found the tow truck driver who fixed the flat and wanted to come to the house after everyone had left the party. Alan has been arrested, but I know that Mike won't be satisfied until they locate this guy and find out where he was the night of the party."

"So what's your point?" Fran asked.

"My point is that twenty-four hours ago we didn't know about Jamie supposedly swimming with Kerry the night of the party. We both are certain he had nothing to do with what happened to Kerry. The police still haven't found the tow truck driver. My point is there's still a lot we don't know. Let's try to reserve judgment."

"Okay. Enough on this topic for now. Let's have a glass of wine."

When they were in the living room sipping their wine, Fran said, "You told us you were going to a seminar with Scott Kimball and that you might have dinner with him. You got home pretty late, so I'm assuming you went to dinner. How was it?"

"The seminar or the dinner?" Aline asked

with a smile.

Fran managed to laugh. "Seminars are all the same. Tell me about the dinner."

"It was actually very nice. It was an Italian restaurant. The food was delicious. I had —"

Her mother cut her off. "I want to hear about Scott Kimball."

"Mom, why am I not surprised? I like Scott. He's a very nice guy, and good-looking as well. He's intelligent and easy to talk to."

But as she was speaking, the memory of sitting across the table from Mike Wilson came to mind. I so much more enjoyed his company, she thought. But now is not the time to say that.

Fran said, "Honey, this is very tough for all of us. But if you have a chance to have an enjoyable evening, I want you to take it. Dad and I are finalizing plans to go to Bermuda for a long weekend. A change of scenery will do us both good."

"I agree. That will be great for *both* of you."

59

Mike reviewed the lab report regarding the analysis of the stain the tech had lifted from the back door of the Chapman home. It was blood. The sample had then been compared to Kerry's DNA, and produced a match. It was definitely Kerry's blood.

Armed with Tony Carter's statement that Jamie told him he had gone swimming with Kerry after her party, and having found Kerry's blood on the back door of the Chapman home, Mike applied for a search warrant. It was granted immediately.

The day had become overcast. The breeze was unusually cool for a September morning. Mike, who loved to go golfing, hoped that this would not be an indication of an early onset of cold weather.

With Andy Nerlino at his side and the search warrant in hand, he rang the front doorbell of the Chapman home. Almost immediately, it was answered. Marge was wearing an apron over a pair of old slacks with bleach marks. She looked startled to see them.

"Mrs. Chapman, you might remember me. My name is Mike Wilson. I'm a detective with the Bergen County Prosecutor's Office. This is my colleague Detective Andy Nerlino."

"Of course I remember you. I'm embarrassed. I'm dressed to clean my house. I didn't know you were coming."

"It's all right, Mrs. Chapman," Mike said. "You're absolutely fine the way you are. I must inform you that we have obtained a warrant from a judge to search your home. Here's your copy."

Stunned as she looked down at the document, Marge said, "I don't get it. Why on earth would you want to search my home?"

Mike replied, "It's in connection with our investigation of Kerry Dowling's murder. And while we're here, we want to speak to both you and your son Jamie. Is he home?"

Her mouth dry, Marge said, "He's upstairs in his room watching TV."

"Detective Nerlino will stay with you here. I'm going upstairs to speak to Jamie."

"Oh, no," Marge said. "Jamie might get upset. I think I should be with him when he speaks to you."

"Your son Jamie is twenty years old. Is that correct?"

"Yes, it is."

"Then he is legally an adult. I'm going to talk to him alone," Mike said as he headed toward the stairs.

Marge reached out her hand as if to stop him. Then she sighed nervously, and walked to the couch. The vacuum cleaner was on the rug. Her foot brushed against it as she sat down. There was a dust cloth and furniture polish on the table. Almost unconsciously, she picked them up and put them down next to the vacuum.

"You remind me of my mother," Andy said. "She goes through the house once a week. There isn't a spot left in it when she's finished. I can tell you're like her."

Marge moistened her lips. "I guess I am. I want to go upstairs and be with Jamie."

"In a little while Detective Wilson will be finished. I'm sorry, but I have to insist that you stay here."

Mike knocked on Jamie's half-closed door. As he pushed it open, he said, "Hi, Jamie, I'm Mike Wilson. Do you remember me?"

Jamie was sprawled across his bed. The movie *Ace Ventura: Pet Detective* was playing in the background. "You work in Hackensack," Jamie said proudly.

"That's right, Jamie. I'm a detective. My office is in Hackensack. Would it be okay if the TV is off when we're talking?"

"Sure. It's a tape. I can watch it whenever I want," Jamie said as he got up and hit the power button on the TV. He went back to his bed and sat on it.

"I like watching movies," Mike said. "Do you?"

"Yes, Mom buys tapes and DVDs for my birthday."

"Your mom is very nice."

"She loves me, and I love her."

"Jamie, do you remember the last time I came and talked to you in your room?"

Jamie nodded.

"You told me Kerry had gone to Heaven."

"She's there with my dad."

"And I told you that the police and Kerry's parents are trying to find out what happened to Kerry before she went to Heaven."

"I remember."

"That's great, Jamie. I'll bet you're really good at remembering things."

Jamie smiled.

"I want you to remember the night Kerry had her party, the night she went to Heaven. I asked if you had seen Kerry in her backyard cleaning up after the party. You know what you told me?"

Mike took out his small notebook and read. You said, "I did not go swimming with Kerry."

"I'm not allowed to talk about this," Jamie said, looking down and avoiding eye contact with Mike.

"Why not, Jamie?"

When he didn't answer, Mike asked, "Who told you you can't talk about this?"

"My mom said it's a secret. You're not supposed to tell secrets."

Mike paused for a moment. "Jamie, your mom said it was okay for me to come up to your room and talk to you. Do you know what else she said?"

"No," he answered as he shook his head.

"She said it's okay for you to tell me the secret. She even told me part of the secret. She said the night of Kerry's party you didn't stay in your room. You went outside. She said you can tell me the rest of the secret."

"Okay," Jamie said softly. "Kerry lets me go swimming with her. She went swimming after her party. I wanted to go swimming, so I went over her house."

"Was Kerry in her pool when you went over?"

"Yes."

"Did you talk to Kerry when you went over?"

"Yes."

"What did you say?"

"I said, 'Kerry, it's Jamie. Let's go swimming.' "

"Jamie, try to remember. This is important. Did Kerry answer you?"

"She said, 'I can't.' "

"Kerry told you, 'I can't go swimming'?"

"She was sleeping in the water."

"Jamie, did you go in the water with Kerry?"

Jamie started to tear up. "I got my new sneakers and my pants wet."

"Did you touch Kerry when she was in the pool?"

Jamie held his hand in the air as if shaking someone. "I said 'Kerry, wake up, wake up.' "

"What did Kerry say?"

"She was still sleeping in the water."

"Jamie, you're doing a really good job at remembering. I have a few more questions. So Kerry kept sleeping in the pool. What did you do then?"

"My sneakers and pants were all wet. I came home and went up to my room."

"Where was your mom when you came home?"

265

"She was sleeping in her chair."

"Where is her chair?"

"In the living room."

"Did you talk to your mom?"

"No. She was sleeping."

"Okay, what did you do when you went to your room?"

"I took off my sneakers and socks and pants. I hid them on the floor of my closet."

"Why did you hide them?"

"Because they were all wet. My sneakers are new. I'm not supposed to get them wet."

Mike stopped for a moment. The information provided by Tony Carter appears to be accurate.

"Jamie, do you know what a golf club is?"

"Mr. Dowling has one."

"The night you went swimming with Kerry after the party, did you see a golf club?"

"I put it on the chair."

"Jamie," Mike said while glancing down at his notebook, "when I came to see you last time, you said you weren't invited to the party. You were older. It was only for the high school kids. Do you remember that?"

"Yes," he said, while looking down.

"When people don't get invited to parties, sometimes they get angry. Were you mad at

266

Kerry when she didn't invite you?"

"I'm her friend."

"I know that Jamie, and sometimes friends can hurt our feelings. When she didn't invite you, were you mad at Kerry?"

"I was sad."

"What do you do when you're sad?"

"I go to my room and watch tapes and DVDs."

Mike decided to change course. "Jamie, do you know Alan Crowley?"

"My mom and I saw him on TV. He kissed Kerry and went home."

"Then what happened, Jamie?"

"Big Guy hit her and pushed her in the pool."

"Do you know who Big Guy is?"

Jamie smiled broadly. "My dad called me Big Guy."

"Jamie, did you hit Kerry?"

"No."

"Did you push her in the pool?"

"No. Big Guy did."

"Jamie, are you Big Guy?"

"Yes."

"Are you the Big Guy who hit Kerry and pushed her in the pool?"

"I'm Big Guy. Big Guy hit Kerry and pushed her in the pool."

"Jamie, you're a Big Guy. Is there anybody

else who's a Big Guy?"

There were footsteps on the stairs. Marge pushed open the door and came in, with Nerlino trailing behind her. "You have no right to keep me away from my son," she said.

She went over and sat beside Jamie. "Are you all right, dear?"

"I told him the secret. You said it was all right."

Marge's glare at Mike Wilson was steely.

Mike stood up. "Mrs. Chapman, as I told you earlier, we have a warrant to search these premises." He looked at Jamie's feet. "Are those your new sneakers, Jamie?"

"Yes. Do you like them?"

"Yes, I do. I'm going to need to borrow them for a few days."

"That's okay," Jamie said. While looking at his mother for approval, he removed his sneakers.

"Jamie, do you remember what clothes you were wearing the night you went swimming with Kerry after her party?"

"Yes, I do. My mom bought the shirt for me."

"Can I see it?"

"Sure," Jamie said as he walked over to the dresser and opened and closed two drawers. "Mom bought it in Disneyworld," he said proudly as he unfolded it and showed it to the detective.

"Do you remember which pants you wore when you went in the pool with Kerry?"

Jamie appeared confused as he looked in his closet. "I have a lot of pants."

"That's okay, Jamie. So that's the shirt you wore in the pool when you went swimming with Kerry?"

"Yes," he said smiling. "It's dry now."

"Did you wash it, Jamie?"

"No, my mom did."

Tony Carter had said that on the Sunday morning he and Jamie talked at the Acme, Jamie had told him that he wasn't wearing his new sneakers because they had gotten wet.

"Jamie, this is Detective Nerlino. Would you bring the shirt and sneakers downstairs? He's going to give you a bag to put them in."

"Okay," Jamie said as he followed Nerlino out of the room.

When they were alone, Marge went on the defensive. "You can ask Father Frank. I was planning to call the police and tell them what Jamie saw. The lawyer Father Frank got for Jamie and me is in Atlanta. I was going to talk to you after I spoke to him in two days. Father Frank is going with me to see the lawyer. Then we can talk."

"Mrs. Chapman, let me be clear. Are you saying that you and Jamie have an attorney?"

"Yes, we have one."

"It's your right to have one."

"I want to talk to him before Jamie or I talk any more to you."

"Okay. There will be no more questions today, but we will be executing the search warrant."

Jamie yelled from downstairs. "It was okay to tell them our secret, right, Mom?"

"Yes, Jamie, it was all right," Marge called back.

Her tone was weary, and she was short of breath as she came down the stairs.

The phone rang. It was Father Frank. "Marge, I'm just calling to check in and make sure you are okay."

60

For Marge, the two days before attorney Greg Barber returned from Atlanta were interminable. She had told Father Frank that Detective Wilson had insisted on talking to Jamie without her being in the room. "I don't know what Jamie told him or how the detective could have twisted it," she said, "but I'm so frightened."

"Marge, the appointment with Greg Barber is the day after tomorrow at ten o'clock. I'll pick you up at nine-thirty and we'll ride over together. Greg is a top-drawer defense lawyer. I can assure you of that. I know you'll feel better after you speak to him."

Jamie intuitively knew she was upset. Three or four times he asked her, "Mom, are you mad at me because I told our secret? Mike said it was all right."

"I'm not angry at you, Jamie," Marge repeated each time. When he asked her that, it reminded her of how trusting he always is, and how easily he could be led when questioned.

As he had promised, Father Frank picked her up promptly at 9:30. "Greg Barber's office is around the corner from the courthouse," he explained.

When they passed the courthouse, Marge looked at it and cringed. This was where they brought Alan Crowley, she thought. She recalled seeing the pictures of him on television in the orange jumpsuit. She imagined Jamie wearing it and couldn't bear the possibility.

They arrived ten minutes early, but the receptionist brought them immediately into Greg Barber's private office.

Marge liked his appearance. He was about fifty years old, with thinning gray hair. His horn-rimmed glasses made him look more like a schoolteacher. He walked out from behind his desk to greet them and motioned them to a small conference table.

After they sat down, Barber came directly to the point. "Mrs. Chapman, Father Frank gave me some information about your son. I understand he has special needs, an intellectual disability?"

Marge nodded, then burst out, "Father Frank and I were planning to go with you to the police and tell them what Jamie saw, but then that blabbermouth Tony Carter started bragging about the fact that he had solved the murder, that my Jamie had killed Kerry Dowling. Because of that, the detective came to our house and insisted on talking to Jamie in his room upstairs while I was downstairs. God only knows what he tricked Jamie into saying."

"Mrs. Chapman, I'm sure you've heard of the Miranda warnings. Did the detective ever tell you or Jamie that you didn't have to speak to him?"

"I don't remember him saying anything about that. I have no idea what he said to Jamie upstairs."

"How old is Jamie?"

"He's twenty."

"Did Jamie go to school?"

"Oh, yes. He went to the local high school, Saddle River. He was in special classes the four years he was there."

"What is the nature of his disability?"

"When he was born, it was a difficult delivery. He was deprived of oxygen. The doctors told us he has brain damage."

"Jamie lives with you now?"

"Of course. He couldn't be on his own."

"Jamie's father?"

"He died when Jamie was fifteen."

"Does Jamie work?"

"Yes. He bags groceries five days a week, four hours a day, at the local Acme. That's where he told Tony Carter that he went swimming with Kerry the night of her party."

"Mrs. Chapman, parents of children who have intellectual disabilities often make a decision around the time the child turns eighteen. To protect the child they apply for a guardianship which makes their child, in the eyes of the law, a permanent child. Did you do this on Jamie's behalf?"

"At school they suggested I apply for a guardianship. I did."

"So you went to the courthouse, appeared in front of a judge, and he granted a full guardianship, you make all decisions for him?"

"Yes, it was a few months after his eighteenth birthday."

"Good. Do you know where your guardianship papers are?"

"I have them at home in the top drawer of my dresser."

Father Frank said, "Marge, give them to me when I drop you off."

"Why do you want them?" she asked Barber.

"Because I want to determine whether the detective had a right to question Jamie outside your presence and without your permission. Beyond that, even though Jamie wasn't under arrest or in police custody, I think I can make a strong argument that, since he was a suspect, he didn't have to speak to the detective.

"But that's for later. Now, let's start from the beginning, with the night your neighbor had a party and the young girl was murdered. Tell me everything you recall about that night and the following morning, right up until when the detectives came to your house last week."

Step by step Marge related everything that had happened. Finding Jamie's wet clothes and sneakers in his closet. Seeing Steve Dowling carry Kerry's body out of the pool. In a panic washing the clothes and sneakers. Making Jamie swear that he wouldn't tell anyone about going in the pool that night. She told Greg Barber about Jamie telling her that he had seen Alan talking to Kerry and then leaving.

And her concern about Jamie saying that the Big Guy hit Kerry and pushed her in the pool, and that she had felt guilty ever since Alan Crowley was arrested.

She finished by saying, "Father Frank will back me up on this. I was planning to go to the police, but I wanted to speak to you first. But then that Tony Carter told everyone that he had solved Kerry's murder and that Jamie did it."

"Mrs. Chapman, there are some circumstances in which I would be concerned that two family members whom the police are scrutinizing should have separate lawyers. I think, however, that for the time being, I can be the attorney for both you and Jamie. Do you have any issue with that?"

"Oh no, Mr. Barber. I know you'll do your best for both of us, but it is Jamie that I am worried about."

"All right, fine. We'll work out the financial details later. For now leave it in my hands."

Barber turned to Father Frank. "Father, when you drop Mrs. Chapman off, would you please leave those guardianship papers in my home mailbox."

"Of course," Father Frank said.

"Mrs. Chapman, I cannot stress strongly enough what I'm about to tell you. If anyone contacts you or Jamie wanting to talk about this case, do not say anything. Just give them my name and phone number and tell them to contact me."

"Mr. Barber —"

"Please call me Greg."

"Greg, I'm so relieved and grateful. Please call me Marge."

He smiled. "Marge, Father Frank speaks very highly of you and your son. We will get through this. I want you to come back tomorrow at one P.M. with Jamie. I need to go through everything with him."

61

After her conversation with Fran, Aline was troubled. She had to speak to Mike Wilson about Jamie, but she knew it would not be a short conversation.

He answered on the first ring. "Mike, it's Aline Dowling. I have some information I want to share with you. By any chance are you free for dinner tonight?"

"Yes, I am" was his immediate response.

"Do you know Esty Street, the restaurant in Park Ridge?"

"Sure. I love their food."

"Seven o'clock tonight?"

"We're on."

For the rest of the afternoon Aline had a sense of relief. She knew Mike Wilson was determined to find Kerry's killer, but he didn't know Jamie the way she did.

When she arrived at the restaurant, Mike was already there. He waved to her from a table in the corner. She slid into her chair and saw a white wine waiting for her. This time there was a white wine in front of Mike as well.

"Tonight I'm joining you," he said.

"If ever I needed a glass of wine, it's now," Aline told him.

"Then I'm glad you didn't have to wait for it. By the way, how are your folks doing?"

"They're doing a little better. They're planning a long weekend in Bermuda."

"Glad to hear that. They've been through a lot."

The waiter came over with menus. "Let's take a look and get our order in before it gets crowded."

He could sense the tension in Aline. Her eyes looked strained, and he realized that in the last few weeks she had lost some weight.

Mike said, "Aline, I asked how your parents are doing. I neglected to ask how you're doing."

"Frankly, Mike, I just can't believe what's going on. I'll be the first to admit I don't know Alan Crowley very well. Most of the time Kerry went out with him I was in London. I met him a few times when I was home for a holiday. But whenever Kerry mentioned him in emails to me, it seemed obvious that she and Alan cared deeply about each other. I know that they had that spat at the party, but there's a big difference between being upset with each other and killing somebody.

"You certainly know that Tony Carter is telling everybody that Jamie killed Kerry. It drives me crazy to hear that. I started babysitting Jamie when he was eight years old. I can tell you right now that there's no way in the world that he ever would hurt Kerry. Quite simply, he loved her."

"Aline, you just admitted to me that you don't really know Alan Crowley that well because you were away during the time Kerry was dating him. Let me remind you, you were also away from Jamie those three years. That sweet young boy you babysat for is now a young man. People change over time. That may be the case with Jamie."

"Mike, people don't change that much. I would swear on a stack of Bibles that Jamie is incapable of hurting anyone, especially Kerry."

"Aline, I'm going to share something with you that I really shouldn't. I want your assurance that this conversation stays at this table."

Aline nodded.

"I went to the Chapman home the other day and talked to Jamie. My office is currently processing several pieces of potential evidence. We'll know a lot more when we get the results."

Aline knew she had to be satisfied with that. "Just to let you know, Mike," she said, "my mother agrees with me that Jamie would never hurt Kerry. And she saw Jamie all the time in the three years I was gone."

"Aline, I want to find out what happened to Kerry. I'm going to pursue every lead to its conclusion."

He decided to change the subject. "What's new at school?"

"The usual. Right now the seniors are under the gun to finish their college application essays. I'm spending a lot of time working on them. As you can imagine, some of them are so torn between what schools to apply to."

"I'm not surprised. This is the first really important decision they're making in their lives."

"I do have one student I'm worried about. She started at the school in January after moving here from Chicago. For no apparent reason her marks have gone down. She's very withdrawn. Her parents are worried sick."

"Do you think drugs are involved?"

"No, I don't. But I can sense she's holding something back. I just don't know what it can be."

"Does she have any friends at school?"

"Even though she's two years younger, she was very close to Kerry when they played lacrosse last spring. I'm told that Kerry was her confidante on the team. And now she misses her very much."

"Are you worried she might hurt herself?"

"Yes, and so are her parents. They tried to get her to see a therapist. She refused."

"Typical, unfortunately. I really hope the problem is homesickness and, with time, she'll get over it."

Their orders came, and Mike was happy that as the meal went on, Aline's spirits brightened considerably.

Mike walked her to her car and opened the door for her. It was an effort to resist the urge to put his arm around her.

62

On Saturday morning when the doorbell rang at Marge's home, she was surprised to see Mike Wilson.

"Mrs. Chapman, I have applied for permission to take Jamie's fingerprints. You and Jamie have the right to appear with your lawyer in court. A hearing is scheduled for Monday morning at ten o'clock, and then the judge will make his decision. Here is your copy of the paperwork."

Visibly flustered, Marge said, "Our lawyer is Greg Barber in Hackensack. He's very smart. I'm gonna call him right now."

"Okay, here's my card. If Mr. Barber wants to contact me before the hearing, he can do so."

As she watched Wilson drive away, Marge was already dialing Greg Barber's number. His secretary connected them and Marge read the document she had been given.

"Marge, let's stay calm. I'm not surprised

by this. Even though Jamie is not under arrest, the judge can order that he submit to fingerprinting. I'll go to court with you and Jamie tomorrow. I'll object, but I'm pretty sure the judge will order it.

"And since we'll be in court tomorrow morning, I want you to bring Jamie to see me tonight at seven."

Monday morning at 10 A.M. Greg Barber appeared in the courtroom of Judge Paul Martinez, ironically the same judge who had arraigned Alan Crowley. Barber was with Marge Chapman, who looked dejected and frightened, and Jamie, who looked excited to be there.

Greg had spent more than an hour speaking to Jamie and Marge the night before. Every instinct in his body told him that Jamie had not committed this crime. Those same instincts, however, told him that Alan Crowley had not committed the crime either.

Barber spoke to the assistant prosecutor, Artie Schulman. He told him that he would object to the application for fingerprints, but he conceded that the judge would probably grant it. He indicated that he represented both Marge and Jamie, and that no one should speak to them without his permission.

During the brief hearing, Schulman put on the record the reasons for the application and the interview of Jamie Chapman. While Chapman's account admittedly was not entirely clear, it would, if true and accurate, exonerate Alan Crowley. It was obvious that the judge was taken aback by this new information. He ordered that Jamie submit to the taking of his fingerprints.

Greg then gently explained to Jamie what would happen when he went downstairs, and that he would be there with him.

Jamie and Marge quietly followed their lawyer as the detective walked them to the Prosecutor's Office on the second floor of the courthouse. Marge waited on a bench outside in the hallway as Greg and Jamie went in.

Within thirty minutes of the end of the hearing, Prosecutor Matthew Koenig was inundated with calls from the media demanding to know more details about Jamie Chapman, the new suspect in Kerry Dowling's murder.

The angriest call he received was from Alan's attorney, Lester Parker. "You know, Prosecutor, I recognize that you can't immediately share every single development in the case. Obviously, your investigation has a long way to go. But I have an innocent eighteen-year-old who is so depressed that his parents are worried he's going to harm himself. When you go into a public courtroom and admit to these developments and I have to hear it from a member of the press, that's just not right, and you know it."

Koenig responded, "Look Lester, I took your call because you deserved an explanation. We were hoping that this would not be picked up by the press until after we got his fingerprints and we see if it helps the investigation one way or the other. We have no obligation to call you unless we come to the conclusion that Alan didn't do it. And we are very far from making that determination. I'm going to end this call now. If anything significant develops, I will let you know."

"And I'll let you know if my innocent client commits suicide while waiting for your call."

63

With Jamie in the car Marge drove directly home from the hearing. They were in the door a few minutes when he said, "Mom, I'm hungry. I want Chinese food for lunch." Marge was about to call to order it and have it delivered when she opened the refrigerator and saw they were out of Diet Coke.

"Jamie, I'll get the Chinese food, and I have to stop at the store. I won't be long. Why don't you watch a movie while I'm gone."

Returning twenty minutes later, Marge drove up her block and was dismayed to see a news truck parked in front of her house. Jamie was on the lawn smiling. A woman with a microphone was standing next to him. A camera was pointed at them.

Marge turned into the driveway and slammed on the brakes. As she got out of the car, she heard Jamie saying, "And then I went swimming with Kerry."

"Leave him alone!" Marge shouted. "Jamie, don't say anything. Get in the house."

Startled at his mother's tone, Jamie ran inside.

With the cameraman struggling to keep up, the reporter hurried over to Marge. "Mrs. Chapman, would you like to comment on today's hearing in Hackensack?"

"No, I won't. I want you and that guy with the camera to get off my property right now," Marge yelled as she opened her front door and slammed it behind her.

Feeling a little better in the safety of her home, but frantic about what else Jamie might have said, Marge collapsed into her favorite chair. How much more of this can I take? she asked herself as she looked around for her purse. She needed a nitroglycerine tablet.

"Mom!" Jamie yelled from upstairs in his room. "Am I gonna be on TV like Alan Crowley?"

"No, Jamie," Marge said, even as she wondered if he would be.

"Mom, I want to eat in my room. Can you bring up the Chinese food?"

Marge realized that along with the Diet Coke and her purse, it was still in the car. She walked over and peeked out the window. The camera crew was gone. The coast was clear. She ran to her car.

64

Assistant Prosecutor Artie Schulman and Mike Wilson walked together into Prosecutor Matt Koenig's office. They informed him that a fingerprint on the golf club had been matched to Jamie Chapman.

"He admitted picking it up and putting it on a chair by the pool," Mike said.

"But we also have Alan Crowley's prints on the weapon. Isn't that right?"

"Yes, we do. We know Alan lied, but later Chapman told us that he saw Crowley talk to the victim and leave the property before anything happened to her."

"I understand Chapman is intellectually impaired. Do you believe the information he provided is credible?" Koenig asked.

Mike sighed. "For the most part, yes. He understood my questions. His memory was clear about going into the pool with the victim. He remembered and quickly provided the clothing he had on that night. His perception was that the victim was asleep in the pool. Of course, that suggests that Kerry Dowling was dead when he arrived on the scene. But he also said that when he asked Kerry to wake up, she said, 'I can't.' If that's literally true, she was still alive."

"Could she have been in the pool, injured, when she said, 'I can't'?"

"No. She had sustained a massive traumatic blow to the back of the head. She would have lost consciousness immediately, before she even hit the water."

"All right. So what is your gut regarding Jamie Chapman?"

"His answers amounted to mixed signals. I asked him if he hit Kerry, and he said no. He said that 'Big Guy' hurt Kerry, and his father called him Big Guy. I tried to pin him down on whether there was another Big Guy at the scene, but I just couldn't get a clear answer. So whether he saw somebody else do it or did it himself, I just don't know."

"So where does that leave us with Alan Crowley, who this office arrested?"

Mike answered, "One thing Jamie was specific about is that he saw Alan Crowley hug the victim and then leave."

Artie, almost sounding defensive, spoke. "Boss, almost everything pointed to Alan

Crowley, and that is why we recommended that you approve his arrest. The latest developments give us great concern as to whether or not he was the killer."

The chagrin on Matt Koenig's face was evident, as the enormity of the arrest of possibly the wrong person sunk in.

"What we need to do is find out everything we can about Jamie Chapman," Artie said. "School records, behavior incidents. Any signs of violence. As a special ed student, he would have had an IEP, an individual education plan. Let's get that, see what it says and talk to the teachers he had along the way."

Koenig said, "You know that will require another court order."

"I know," Artie said.

"And you know Chapman's lawyer could fight us every step of the way. But you know, ironically, he might agree to let us have these records if he thinks they will help his client."

"All right," Artie said, "I'll get in touch with Greg Barber and see what his position is."

65

The morning following the court hearing and the press firestorm, Artie Schulman, Matt Koenig and Mike met again. The three men knew that they had come to an impasse.

The once almost ironclad case against Alan Crowley was collapsing. Jamie Chapman, while probably not the killer, could not be completely ruled out. He had spoken about a Big Guy hurting Kerry, and they didn't know if he was referring to himself or someone else. Both Crowley and Chapman had attorneys who had directed that there would be no more interviews of their clients.

And the nagging loose end about the driver who had changed Kerry's flat tire still lingered.

Koenig was correct in his prediction that Greg Barber would not oppose their receiving copies of Jamie's school records. Barber had just gone through the set he had received from Jamie's schools. He had his secretary copy and deliver them to the Prosecutor's Office.

The records showed, as they'd expected, a young man with severe cognitive impairment. They also revealed a history in school of being compliant and friendly, and with no hint of violence or aggressive behavior.

They all agreed that they were not at the point of requesting to a court that the criminal complaint against Alan Crowley be dismissed. Matt Koenig somberly added that he would contact Lester Parker and tell him that he would agree that the electronic bracelet be removed and the travel restrictions outside New Jersey be lifted. He knew this wouldn't placate Parker for long, but he would tell him that's as far as he was willing to go now.

Koenig ended the meeting by saying, "I know we're all doing our utmost to solve this case. We just have to take the heat that comes with it."

66

It had been two and a half weeks since Kerry's death. A sad sense of finality was settling in. Aline made an effort to be home most nights by six-thirty. She wanted to be there to have a glass of wine with her mother. She believed that their chats brightened Fran's spirits. But tonight when she came in, it was obvious that her mother was having a very dark day. Her eyes were swollen. She was sitting in the living room sifting through a family photo album.

When Fran saw her come in, she looked up but left the book open. "Do you remember how Kerry broke her ankle when she was eleven? I kept warning and warning her. She was a good ice skater. But she couldn't do those twirls the way she wanted to. But she always kept on trying."

"I remember," Aline said. "I was never any good at ice skating."

"No, you weren't," her mother agreed.

"You were always the great student. Kerry was the great athlete."

"I think it's time for a glass of wine," Aline suggested as she lifted the photo album off her mother's lap.

Fran closed her eyes. "I guess so," she said indifferently.

Aline went to the kitchen and called out, "Something smells really delicious in here."

"It's veal parmigiana. I thought it would taste good for a change."

Aline did not have to be reminded that veal parmigiana had been Kerry's favorite. She came back with the two glasses of wine and turned on several more lights. "Brighten the corner where you are," she said.

"I'm surprised you know that song. It's an old gospel favorite."

"Mom, I don't know the song. I do know that every time you turn on a light, you say that."

Fran smiled a real smile. "I guess I do." Then she added, "Aline, I don't know what your father and I would have done if you had stayed in London."

"I would have come straight home."

"I know you would have. Now let's change the subject. How was school today?"

"I told you how all the seniors are fixated on which colleges to apply to. When it

296

comes to writing the essays, some of them have a natural ability. They can effortlessly tell a story. For others, every word on the page is a struggle."

The sound of the front door opening announced Steve's arrival. He walked into the living room, looked at their glasses of wine and said, "I guess it's five o'clock somewhere in the world."

He leaned over and put his arms around Fran. "How are you doing?"

"Today was rough. I was out running errands and drove past the high school. The girls' soccer team was practicing. It got me thinking."

"I know. I make it a point to not drive past the high school. Is there any wine left, or did you two drink it all?"

"I'll get you one, Dad," Aline said.

When Aline was in the kitchen, the doorbell rang.

"Are we expecting anyone?" Steve asked as he got up.

"No," Fran told him.

As Aline walked back into the living room with her father's glass of wine, Steve came into the room with Scott Kimball at his side. What is he doing here? Aline asked herself.

"Hi, Scott. This is a surprise. You've obviously met my father. This is my mother,

Fran. Mom, this is Scott Kimball."

"I know who he is," Fran said. "Scott was Kerry's lacrosse coach."

"Scott, anything to drink?" Steve asked.

"I'll join you folks in a white wine, if that's okay."

"Take that one," Steve said, pointing to the glass in Aline's hand. "I'll get myself another."

"Do sit down," Fran said.

And why not take your shoes off? Aline thought.

"So Scott," Aline asked, "what brings you over?"

"Aline, I tried to phone you. I guess your phone was off. This afternoon a friend of mine called me. He's heartbroken. He has two tickets for *Hamilton* tomorrow night, but he has to leave in the morning on a business emergency and gave them to me. I was hoping you might be free."

"Oh, Aline, how wonderful," Fran said. "Your father and I have been dying to see that show."

Aline wondered if there was any way she could persuade Scott to give the tickets to her parents. She hesitated, trying to find a way to say no.

Fran answered for her. "Oh, Aline, of

course you'll go. Everyone raves about that show."

Steve said, "Scott, that is so nice of you."

Aline really did want to see *Hamilton*. She just didn't like the idea of spending a third evening with Scott Kimball. She really resented the fact that he had just walked in. Before she could answer, her mother said, "Scott, do you like veal parmigiana?"

"I *love* veal parmigiana, but I don't want to intrude."

"Anyone who comes bearing two tickets to *Hamilton* certainly is not intruding," Steve said heartily. "Right, Aline?"

There was nothing she could do but say, "Of course not."

Scott was seated in the chair opposite her, where Kerry used to sit.

At dinner he brought up the subject of his family. "I was raised in Nebraska. My mother and father are still there. So are my grandparents. I spend all the holidays with them. But as I mentioned to Aline, I love to travel. Most summers I'm on the road."

"We go on a river cruise once a year with friends," Fran said. "I thoroughly enjoy them. Last year it was the Danube. The year before that the Seine."

"A river cruise is next on my list," Scott

299

said. "Which line did you use?"

Aline was quiet through dinner. Next thing you know he'll say he has two tickets to a river cruise, she thought. Plan on inviting somebody else.

Over coffee she wondered why she resented Scott so much. She had not intended to go out with him a second time, but she had to admit she had enjoyed herself. She appreciated how concerned he was about Valerie.

Aline did not want to be manipulated into a dating situation. She would finish dinner tonight, go to *Hamilton* tomorrow and then that would be it. Period.

Then the thought of Mike came into her mind. If he had come in with those tickets, she would have been delighted to say yes.

She knew she was right when the next night, after seeing *Hamilton,* Scott drove her home, and walked her to the door. As she fished her key from her purse, he suddenly put his arms around her and kissed her. "I'm falling in love with you, Aline," he said. "Make that 'have fallen' in love with you."

She broke away from the embrace and put her key in the lock, turned it and opened the door. "Do us both a favor. Don't," she said emphatically, as she stepped in and closed the door behind her.

67

Mike was barely in his office when Investigator Sam Hines knocked on the half-opened door. "Mike, I think I might have something on that tow truck driver we're looking for."

Mike waved him in, pointing to a chair opposite his desk. "What have you got?"

"It's a bit of a fluke I found this, because I wasn't even looking for it. I've been researching drivers who work for the tow truck companies that have permits to operate in local municipalities. So far, nothing interesting has turned up. But these companies aren't the only ones that own tow trucks. Junkyards typically have one to retrieve wrecks."

"That makes sense."

"So that's what made this arrest report from the Lodi Police Department so interesting." Hall began summarizing. "Twenty-four-year-old Edward Dietz was arrested three hours ago and charged with possession of cocaine and drug paraphernalia. He was stopped on Route 17 for speeding and passing on the right. The tow truck he was driving was registered to Ferranda Brothers, an auto salvage company in Moonachie.

"Here's where it gets interesting. I'm reading about this guy they arrested and my phone rings. It's Patrolman Sandy Fitchet from the Lodi police force. Fitchet was aware of the BOLO we put out on the tow truck driver." Mike knew that BOLO was shorthand for "Be On the Look Out" for. "Fitchet said they've been holding this guy while doing an outstanding warrants check, and he has several. Failure to appear in court for a traffic infraction, he's behind in child support, and he had an assault charge against him dropped three months ago, for trying to kiss a woman he had helped in the Woodbury Commons mall parking lot when her car wouldn't start."

"Why was it dropped?"

"The victim was from out of state. She didn't show up to testify."

"How old was the victim?"

"Seventeen."

"So he likes hitting on young women. He offers to help them, and then he tries to take advantage. Nice work, Sam. I want to

302

have a talk with our Good Samaritan right now."

"I had a feeling you would," Hines said. "Fitchet is at the station waiting for you. Dietz is still in their holding cell."

As Mike inched along on Route 17 South, he was fervently hoping that this tow truck driver would be the one who had the encounter with Kerry. On the other hand he could only imagine the field day the press would have if it was revealed that the Prosecutor's Office had a third independent suspect in the Dowling murder. Don't get ahead of yourself, he thought. Odds are this isn't the guy we're looking for.

When he finally arrived at the Lodi police station, the desk sergeant pointed him to a room where Patrolman Sandy Fitchet was seated at a table. Several clear plastic bags were on top of it. One contained a wallet, a pocketknife and keychain. Another was stuffed with papers.

As it turned out, *Patrolman* Fitchet was *Patrolwoman* Fitchet. She stood up, extended her hand and introduced herself. Mike guessed Fitchet was in her mid- to late twenties.

She briefed Mike on the circumstances under which she had pulled over and arrested Dietz. "I'm just starting to go through his personal effects," she said as she spilled the contents of one of the bags out on the table.

"That is one really fat wallet," Mike observed. "Do you mind if I go through it?"

"Be my guest," Sandy said as she started to open another bag filled with papers.

"What are all those?" Mike asked, referring to the bag in front of Sandy.

"This stuff was in his truck. The crack pipe was resting on top of it. Just want to see if there's anything interesting."

"Obviously you searched his truck. How did you get a warrant so quickly?"

"Didn't need one. It's not Dietz's truck. It's registered to Ferranda Brothers. I spoke to the owner. After assuring me that anything I find in the truck doesn't belong to him, he gave me permission to search."

"What is your impression of Dietz?"

"I'm right in the middle of reading him his rights while I'm arresting him, and this jerk starts telling me how beautiful I am. What a creep."

Mike smiled as he listened. Dietz's wallet was so thick Mike wondered if it would fit in his back pocket. He began taking out pieces of paper and sorting them into piles. Wendy's, Dunkin' Donuts and McDonald's receipts. Gas and ShopRite receipts. A traffic summons from two weeks ago. A receipt from a motorcycle repair shop. Several business cards, including one from a doctor and two from attorneys. Mike knew one of the lawyers, whose office was in East Rutherford.

His attention was suddenly riveted by a torn envelope with a phone number scribbled on it.

Sandy must have noticed his expression change. "Mike, what is it?"

Without answering, he pulled his notebook from his pocket and flipped the pages. He glanced back at the number on the torn envelope. A grim smile came over his face.

"Pay dirt," he said. "The number on this piece of paper that came from Dietz's wallet is the cell phone number of Kerry Dowling. He's the guy we've been looking for."

"Mike, when you question Dietz, mind if I watch from the other room?"

"Not at all."

While waiting in another meeting room for Dietz to be brought in, Mike phoned Artie Schulman. The assistant prosecutor insisted Mike call him immediately after he questioned Dietz.

The door opened, and Sandy Fitchet had her hand on Dietz's elbow as she escorted him into the room. He was wearing faded, greasy blue jeans and scuffed work boots. His oil-stained gray T-shirt had a small tear by the right shoulder and the logo of an engine company on the front. His hands were cuffed in front of him. His bare arms showed the telltale welts of recent needle marks. He settled into the folding chair opposite Mike.

Dietz was about five-foot-ten with a crew cut. Despite the fact that he was unshaven and the darkness under his eyes, his features were handsome.

"Mr. Dietz, my name is Mike Wilson. I'm a detective with the Bergen County Prosecutor's Office."

"My name is Eddie Dietz, but you probably already know that. It's an honor to meet you, Detective," he said sarcastically.

"Okay, Eddie, I don't want to take up too much of your valuable time, so let's cut to the chase. Let me begin by saying I have zero interest in your recent speeding ticket, your drug arrest, your outstanding warrants and your overdue child support. I hope I didn't leave anything out. I'm here to talk about one of my cases involving a young woman. Do you know a Kerry Dowling?"

Dietz paused for a moment. "No, that name doesn't ring a bell."

"Maybe this will help," Mike said as he pulled a picture of Kerry out of an envelope and slid it across the table in front of Dietz.

He stared at it, then looked up at Mike and said, "Sorry, don't know her."

"You said you don't *know* her. Are you saying you never met her?"

Dietz shook his head.

"All right, Eddie, let's see if I can improve your memory. The girl in the picture is eighteen-year-old Kerry Dowling. Two and a half weeks ago, after having her high school friends over for a beer party, she was found dead in the swimming pool in her backyard."

"Oh, yeah, I think I might have seen something about that case on TV."

Mike pulled a bag from under his chair and laid it on the table. Pointing to the wallet in the bag, Mike asked, "Is that yours?"

"It looks like mine."

"It is yours, Eddie. And the papers stuffed inside the wallet, they're yours too, aren't they?"

"Maybe."

"Eddie, I want to know about this piece of paper," he said as he put the torn envelope on the table in front of him.

307

"It's somebody's phone number. So what?"

"Eddie, let's cut the crap. About a week before she died, you were on Route 17 in Mahwah. You pulled over and changed a flat tire for Kerry Dowling. You made arrangements with her to provide the alcohol for her upcoming party, a party you wanted to be invited to. You even asked her if you could come by after the party. When she said no, you tried to force yourself on her."

"I didn't force anything. She wanted it."

"Oh, I'm sure she did, Eddie. Just like the girl at Woodbury Commons. A good-looking guy like you helps her get her car started. She just wanted to show her appreciation."

"That's right."

"Eddie, much as I would love to nail you for groping Kerry after you delivered the alcohol, and providing alcohol to a minor, I can't do that. The only witness, Kerry Dowling, is dead, murdered. But that's not the end of the story with you and Kerry, is it? Later that night, you —"

"Wait a minute. You don't think I —"

"Yes, Eddie, I think you went back to her house after the party. Maybe you were a little drunk or high. When she refused your advances, you got really angry and killed her."

Eddie was breathing hard. His eyes, which were dull and listless earlier, were now sharp and focused. "The day she died, that was Saturday night?"

"Saturday, August 25," Mike replied. "The same day you gave her the beer and asked if you could come to the party."

"Okay, I admit it. When I brought her the beer, I asked about going to the party. But I can prove I didn't go to her house that night."

"How? Where were you?" Mike demanded.

"I drove down to Atlantic City that night. I stayed at the Tropicana. I gambled most of the night."

"What time did you get to the Tropicana?"

"I checked in around ten o'clock."

Mike quickly did the math. Atlantic City was 140 miles from Saddle River. Even if Dietz was really pushing it, it would have taken him over two hours to get there. If he murdered Kerry at 11:15, the earliest he could have gotten to the Tropicana was about 1:30 A.M.

"In that garbage pail that you call a wallet, I didn't see a receipt for the Tropicana."

"I don't save everything."

"Did you drive to Atlantic City?"

"Yes."

"Alone?"

"Yes."

"Whose car?"

"Mine."

"Do you have an E-ZPass?"

"Not since I lost my credit card. I pay cash for my tolls."

"How did you pay for your hotel room?"

"Cash."

"Okay, Eddie, I'm gonna check out your Tropicana story. I know where to find you if I need you."

As Mike walked quickly toward the door, the desk sergeant called out to him. "Detective, Officer Fitchet asks if you could wait a few minutes. She wants to talk to you before you leave."

"Okay," Mike said as he moved over to a chair and sat down. He dialed Artie Schulman, who picked up on the first ring. "Artie, I'm still at the Lodi police station. The guy they picked up is the tow truck driver we've been looking for. He's claiming he was in Atlantic City at the time of the murder. I'm checking his story."

"Good work. I'll ask if we have any contacts here that can move things along more quickly. Keep me posted."

Out of the corner of his eye Mike spotted

Sandy Fitchet heading toward him with a piece of paper in her hand. She took the seat next to him. "I just spoke to my uncle, Herb Phillips. He's a lieutenant with the State Police in South Jersey. He works closely with security people at the casinos. Uncle Herb said he and the Tropicana's director of security can meet you or one of your people tomorrow morning at ten to look at surveillance footage. Here are their phone numbers."

"I'm in court tomorrow morning. I can't go myself. I'll send one of my investigators. I owe you a dinner. Thanks so much," Mike said as he hurried out to his car.

His first call was to Sam Hines. After briefing him on the Dietz questioning, Mike said, "Set your alarm. You need to be in Atlantic City by ten o'clock. Call Artie and fill him in."

Mike was in his office the next morning doing paperwork. A delay at the trial had pushed his testimony to the afternoon. When his phone rang at eleven-thirty, the ID screen showed Tropicana Hotel. He picked it up.

"Sam, what have you got?"

"Reservations records show a single room for the night of August 25 booked by a Mr.

311

Edward Dietz. The room was paid for in advance with cash. Security footage shows a young white male who I'm absolutely certain is Dietz entering the hotel at 9:49 P.M. There's more footage I can go through from inside the casino but —"

"Don't bother," Mike said. "If he's in AC at almost ten, there's no way he's back in Saddle River at eleven-fifteen. Thank the guys down there for me."

Mike hung up the phone and exhaled. He was not looking forward to telling Assistant Prosecutor Artie Schulman and Prosecutor Matt Koenig that once again their only suspects in the Dowling murder were Alan Crowley and Jamie Chapman.

68

Marina Long had begun to worry about whether she should give up her job. She had always had a flair for fashion and had gone to work at a dress shop in nearby Ridgewood. She had an innate sense for helping customers choose the right style for their body type and personality. She already had a number of regular customers.

It was a job she had found shortly after she moved to New Jersey. She liked it, and it paid reasonably well. But now her concern about Valerie had deepened. Her daughter's mood over the last few days was even more somber; she was even more detached, if that was possible. The change convinced Marina she should be there in the afternoons when her daughter got home from school.

Everything she said to Valerie seemed to upset her. Marina decided that it would be better to bring up the subject by saying, "I've decided I want a job with different hours, and I'm going to start looking around."

As usual Valerie's response was "Whatever," dismissing the subject.

On Friday morning, when Valerie didn't come down the stairs to breakfast, Marina went up to her room. Valerie was in bed, curled up in a fetal position, sound asleep.

An instinctive sense that something was wrong made Marina rush to her bedside. A prescription jar was on the night table. The cap was off. Marina picked it up. It was her prescription for Ambien, the sleep aid she used occasionally. The jar was empty.

She shook Valerie's shoulder and flipped her over onto her back as she called her name. She did not stir.

Marina looked down at her. She was very pale and her lips were blue. Her breathing was shallow.

"Oh, my God no!" she screamed as she grabbed the phone and dialed 911.

69

Fran and Steve left for Bermuda before lunch on Friday morning. They had decided to extend their trip to a full week. Aline was glad that her mother agreed to the extension. She could see that Fran was getting more and more depressed and desperately needed to get away.

When she returned home from work on Friday, she remembered to bring in the mail. She stopped at the box at the end of the driveway, pulled it out and dropped it on the kitchen table. An envelope addressed to Ms. Kerry Dowling caught her eye. It was from MasterCard.

Aline remembered her parents giving her a credit card just before she had left for college. "For emergencies only," her father had said with a smile, knowing his idea of what constituted an emergency would differ from hers. They must have done the same for Kerry.

Ordinarily she would have left the envelope for them. With her parents away, she decided to open it.

There were only two entries on the bill. ETD, a tire service center. That had to have been the new tire Dad had told Kerry to get, Aline thought.

The second entry was for Coach House, a diner in Hackensack. The charge was $22.79. That's odd, Aline thought. There are diners in Waldwick and Park Ridge, both a lot closer to Saddle River. Why did Kerry go all the way to Hackensack?

When she looked at the date Kerry had gone to the diner, her eyes widened. It was August 25, the day of her party, the day she had been murdered.

Aline pulled out her cell phone and opened her text messages file. The text about something "VERY IMPORTANT" was sent to her at 11:02 A.M. on the same day.

She looked at the bill again. Almost twenty-three dollars is a lot for one person. Kerry might have met somebody for breakfast and picked up the check. Shortly thereafter, she sent me the text. Could there be a connection?

Kerry went to the diner on a Saturday morning. Tomorrow is Saturday. Odds are the same waitstaff will be there, including whoever waited on Kerry.

Who could she have met? Maybe it was Alan. Or if it was one of Kerry's girlfriends, maybe one of the girls on the lacrosse team, I want to talk to her.

Aline went to her computer. She opened Kerry's Facebook page and began to print some of the photos.

This might be a waste of time, she thought, but it could be important to know what Kerry was doing the last day she was alive.

The thought that she might have a chance to discover what was *very important* kept Aline up most of the night.

At quarter past eight she got up, showered and dressed. By eight-forty-five she was in her car headed toward the Coach House. She had skipped her usual light breakfast and coffee. They might be more talkative if I have breakfast there.

She was happy to see that there were only a handful of cars in the parking lot. Two waiters were serving those eating at the counter. Aline looked around. If Kerry was having a private conversation with somebody, she would have chosen a table for two as far away from the other diners as possible. Probably one of the tables to the right

317

or to the left that are up against the windows.

The man behind the register asked, "How many in your party?"

"Just one," she said. "I'd like a table over by the window."

"Sure," he said. "Sit anywhere you want."

A minute after she was seated, a waitress came over carrying a menu. "Can I start you with coffee, honey?"

"Absolutely."

Aline opened the folder that contained the pictures she had printed.

When the waitress returned with the coffee, Aline said, "Obviously you work on Saturdays. Were you working on Saturday, August 25, in the morning?"

The waitress considered. "Let me see. That was three weeks ago. Yes, I was back from vacation. I worked that Saturday."

"My sister ate here that Saturday morning. She met somebody for breakfast. I'm trying to find out who she met. Would you mind looking at some pictures?"

"Sure," she said.

Aline spread several pictures on the table. "That girl," the waitress said, "looks real familiar. I know I've seen her." She was pointing at Kerry.

"That's my sister," Aline said.

"Oh my God," the waitress gasped. "Is she the poor girl who got murdered in the pool?"

"I'm afraid so," Aline said quietly.

"I waited on them that day. They sat at the same table you're sittin' at right now."

The waitress leaned over and stared at one picture after another. She then studied the photo of the lacrosse team and pointed her finger. "That's her. That's the one who was crying."

She was pointing at Valerie.

70

Marge was surprised when the phone rang as she was clearing the breakfast dishes. It was Gus Schreiber, Jamie's manager at Acme.

Puzzled as to why he was calling, she immediately said, "Oh, Mr. Schreiber, you have been so nice to Jamie. He loves working for you. I don't know what he would do if he didn't have his job at the Acme."

There was an uncomfortable silence. Then Schreiber said, "Mrs. Chapman, that's why I'm calling you. At Acme customers are our top priority. A number of them have come to me and expressed their concern about Jamie working in our store under the present circumstances. I hope you'll understand what I mean."

"No, I don't understand. Please explain to me what you mean."

"Mrs. Chapman, after what happened to Kerry Dowling, when Jamie is in the store, people are understandably nervous."

"Tell them they should worry about your other employee, that blabbermouth Tony Carter," Marge said fiercely. "You know damn well Jamie has always been a wonderful employee. That hasn't changed in the two years he's been with you. Now you want to fire him for no good reason. You should be ashamed of yourself."

"Mrs. Chapman, there are a lot of grocery stores around here where people can shop. I have to listen to the concerns of our customers."

"Even if it means being completely unfair to a very loyal employee. As soon as I get off the phone, I'm going to cut my Acme card in half. And let me tell you right now, Jamie has a very good lawyer, and he's going to hear about this conversation!" She slammed down the phone.

Marge could hear Jamie's footsteps as he descended the stairs. He came down dressed for work. "Mom, I'm going now. I'll see you later."

"Hold on, Jamie. I have to talk to you. Sit down. Please."

"Mom, I don't want to be late. I punch in at work."

Marge scrambled to find the right words. "Jamie, sometimes businesses like Acme don't have enough customers. When that happens, they have to tell some of the workers that they can't keep working there."

"Does that mean they're going to fire some of my friends?"

"Yes, it does Jamie. Not just some of your friends. You can't work there anymore either."

"I can't work there? But Mr. Schreiber said I'm one of his best workers."

"I know he did, and he's very sorry," Marge said with a grimace.

Jamie turned around and started toward the stairs. When he neared the top, Marge heard him burst into tears.

71

Mike was in his condo late Saturday morning after he had run some errands. He did not relish the drive he would make to New Brunswick later this evening, but it was the only time the witnesses in another case could meet with him.

He knew it was unprofessional for him to set up a meeting with Aline simply because he wanted to see her. He recalled one of his mother's favorite quotes: "The heart has reasons of which reason knows nothing." He remembered that ever since he was a child, his mother would say that if two unlikely people got together.

The night before, he had been out to dinner with a woman he had dated casually, but regularly, while they were in law school. She was attractive and smart. He had enjoyed her company. But she had never given him the feeling he experienced when he was with Aline.

He reminded himself that his job was to investigate the murder of a young woman. His interaction with the victim's family, including her sister, should be no more than what was necessary to pursue the case.

Despite that, Aline Dowling was very much in his thoughts. He found himself trying to think of reasons related to the case that would make it appropriate for him to call her and suggest that they meet.

Her image was always in his mind. Her hazel eyes, large with long lashes that framed them, sometimes seemed to reflect the color she was wearing. The first time they were out, she had on a violet blue jacket with matching slacks that showed the elegance of her body and carriage. Sometimes she wore her hair loose around her shoulders. That was when her resemblance to Kerry was unmistakable. Other times her hair was caught up at the back of her head. Mike found himself trying to decide which way he liked it best.

She had told him about her fiancé being killed by an intoxicated driver four years ago. He had the sense that there was no one in her life right now. Her heartfelt defense of Jamie Chapman showed her absolute loyalty to someone who was an active suspect in her sister's murder. In her talks with Kerry's friends she was constantly trying to find any clue that might help the investigation find answers.

Besides her reaction to the growing suspicions about Jamie Chapman, it was also clear to him that even though Alan Crowley was under arrest, Aline was not convinced that he was the killer. Whoever murdered Kerry had dealt her a vicious blow to the back of her head. If it was not Jamie or Alan, it meant that a third party who could do that to an eighteen-year-old girl would stop at nothing to escape detection. He knew that Aline was deeply concerned about a student who had been very close to Kerry and was now depressed. Aline had been careful to avoid referring to her by name, so Mike realized she would probably not say much about her to him.

His cell phone rang, and he saw the name on the screen. He grabbed it and said, "Hello Aline."

"Mike, weeks ago you asked me to keep thinking about what Kerry was referring to when she texted that she had something *very important* to talk to me about. I might have made some progress."

"What is it, Aline?" Mike asked quickly.

"Kerry sent that text at 11:02 A.M. I saw on her credit card bill that she went to a diner that morning and met someone for breakfast. The waitress remembered Kerry clearly and said the girl she was with had been crying. I brought pictures of Kerry's friends. She immediately identified who was at the breakfast with Kerry."

"Who is it?"

"The name won't mean anything to you. It's Valerie Long. She's the one I told you about. She played on the lacrosse team with Kerry. From what I understand Kerry had taken her under her wing, and she's heartbroken about Kerry's death. Judging from the time element, Kerry sent me that text very shortly after the breakfast ended."

"Do you have any idea what they spoke about?"

"No, but I'm going to find a reason to get Valerie into my office on Monday and see if she'll talk about it."

"Aline, if that girl said anything to Kerry that might have revealed something tied into her death, it could be very dangerous for you. My suggestion is that you call the girl into your office, tell her that you know that she had breakfast that morning with Kerry and try to make her understand that Kerry was going to tell you whatever it was that she and Valerie discussed. Tell her that Kerry intended to tell you about the conversation and that Kerry would want her to share it with you at your meeting. We can talk about whether it makes sense for me to interview this girl."

"That's what I want to do," Aline said. "Thank you, Mike."

"Aline, I've enjoyed the times we've had dinner together. When this case is over —"

"Yes," Aline interrupted, "I want you to ask me out."

72

On Sunday morning, after the ten o'clock Mass, Aline had made breakfast and was enjoying the peace and quiet as she read the papers. She found herself putting off the work she had brought home from school. One more cup of coffee, she thought, and then an hour at the gym, and then I'll plow through it.

As she was getting up from the table, the home phone rang. The caller ID showed "Private." She picked it up.

"Aline Dowling, is that you?"

"Yes, it is. Who's calling?"

"Aline, this is Marina Long. I'm so sorry to call you at home, and I don't have your cell number."

"Absolutely no problem, Marina. I was thinking about you and Valerie the other day. She wasn't in school on Friday. Is everything okay?"

There was a pause before Marina answered. "No, well yes, things are better now."

"Marina, I can tell you're upset. What happened?"

"Valerie tried to take her life on Friday —"

"Oh, my God, is she all right?"

"Yes, I was in the hospital with her all day Friday. They kept her overnight. A hospital psychiatrist came and spoke to her the next morning. He said it was okay for us to bring her home. She slept most of yesterday and seems to be doing better today. I'm so worried about her. I think she might need to stay home and rest a few more days."

"Marina, don't worry about that. I'll work things out with her teachers. Do you mind if I come to visit her? I can do it right now. I promise I'll only stay a few minutes."

"I know how concerned you are. Of course, stop over."

A ghostly pale Valerie was propped up on the couch in the den with pillows behind her, a blanket covering her. Aline went over, hugged her and pulled up a chair.

"Valerie, we're all so worried about you. If anything had happened to you, our hearts would have been broken. I just want you to know that we love you dearly and want to help you in any way we can. If you ever need someone to talk to, I'm here for you."

Valerie looked at her. "Don't you understand? I can't talk to you," she cried fiercely as she looked away.

Aline went back home. As soon as she was in the door, she called Mike. Unable to reach him, she left a message about visiting Valerie after her suicide attempt.

After returning from a jog around Schlegel Lake, Mike listened to his messages. He immediately tried to call Aline, who didn't pick up. He wasn't sure why, but every instinct told him that Kerry's breakfast meeting with Valerie was somehow linked to what would happen to Kerry that night.

Time is of the essence, he thought. Two suspects are twisting in the wind waiting for this case to be resolved. He searched online and found a listing, including the street address, for a Long in Saddle River. There was only one.

He called the colleague he wanted to come with him. Yes, she could meet him there later if he was able to set it up.

Twenty minutes later Mike's cell phone rang. It was Aline. "Sorry I missed your call. I left my phone at home when I went to the gym."

"Aline, I'm getting very worried that Kerry's death may have had something to do with that breakfast meeting with Valerie at the diner. Especially since this kid has now tried to kill herself. I don't want to wait another minute. A female detective can meet me there. She is very sensitive and experienced. I'm asking you to call Valerie's parents and see if I can go to their home later today. They trust you. I think it would be better if you make the phone call."

"I'll call right now and get right back to you."

Ten minutes later Aline called back. "Mike, it took a little persuading because they feel Valerie is so fragile. They agreed that you could come at six tonight as long as you stop right away if she gets too upset."

"Aline, thanks so much. I owe you a dinner. How about tonight, seven-thirty, eight o'clock? I'll come straight from Valerie's."

"We're on."

73

Looking forward to seeing Mike, Aline showered and went to her closet. She chose a navy-blue silk blouse over fitted jeans. She had just finished her makeup when her phone rang. The name on the screen surprised her. "Hello, Mrs. Chapman."

"Is this Aline Dowling?"

"Yes, it is."

"Aline, my name is Brenda Niemeier. I'm a close friend of Marge's. This is her phone. She asked me to call you."

"Is Mrs. Chapman okay?"

Aline heard the woman fighting off tears as she spoke. "I'm over at Pascack Valley Hospital. It looks like Marge had a heart attack. She had instructions in her pocketbook that I should be called in an emergency and help make decisions if she can't."

"Oh my God," Aline said. Part of her was not surprised. She could only imagine the strain Marge must have been under these past weeks. "Brenda, what can I do to help?"

"When I saw Marge before they took her in for surgery, she was so worried about Jamie. She asked if you could go over and be with him for a little while. Tell him everything will be all right. Maybe help him fix something for dinner. Marge is so worried that if anything happens to her now, who will be there for Jamie?"

"Tell Marge of course I will. Please call me as soon as you get any updates on her condition."

"I will, honey. Marge always told me how nice your family is, and how lucky she is to have you as neighbors."

Aline said goodbye, disconnected and immediately called Mike. She told him about Marge being in the hospital. "I'm going over to spend some time with Jamie. Meet me later at the Chapman house."

"Okay, but meet me outside. Remember, I'm not allowed to talk to Jamie anymore."

74

While driving to Valerie's home, Mike called Detective Angela Walker, who was also en route. He explained the sequence of events that began with finding Kerry in her family pool. Mike told her that he strongly believed something had happened at the breakfast the morning of Kerry's death that resulted in her sending Aline the *very important* text immediately afterward.

There was a specific reason Mike had reached out to Angela. An African American woman who had just turned forty, she had an extraordinary ability to push the right buttons to get young people to talk. He had personally observed her toughness in staring down an eighteen-year-old drug dealer during an interrogation and her incredible compassion when talking to a ten-year-old boy who had witnessed his parents' murder. If there was a way to get Valerie to open up, she would find it.

Marina Long greeted them at the door. She showed them into the den where Valerie was sitting up on a couch with two pillows behind her back and a blanket over her. "Wayne and I will be in the other room if you need us," Marina said as she left.

Mike and Angela settled in the two chairs opposite Valerie. Her eyes looked puffy and sad. After briefly making eye contact with him and Angela, she stared straight ahead.

"Valerie," Mike said, "let me begin by asking, how you are doing?"

"I'm okay," she said quietly.

"This is Detective Angela Walker. She's working with me on the Kerry Dowling case."

Valerie continued to stare straight ahead.

"Valerie," Mike said, "I know that Kerry Dowling was your friend. I know how terrible it is to lose a friend. I'm sure that you want whoever hurt Kerry to be brought to justice."

She continued to stare off into the distance, but her face grew harder.

"Valerie, at eleven o'clock in the morning on the day Kerry died, she sent a text to her sister Aline, who was in England at the time. Kerry said she had something very important to talk to her about. She sent that text right after she had breakfast at the

Coach House diner in Hackensack. Did you have breakfast with Kerry that morning?"

"No," Valerie said as she pulled the blanket higher, almost to her neck.

"Valerie, the waitress at the diner was shown pictures of Kerry's friends. She identified you as the girl who was with Kerry."

Valerie shook her head back and forth as tears began to form in her eyes. Her breathing became heavier. Her hands were balled into fists.

Mike was about to ask another question when he felt Angela's hand on his arm. He knew without being told that it was her signal that she wanted to take over.

"Valerie, honey, would you mind if I sit with you on the couch? I like being close to people when I talk to them."

Without waiting for an answer, Angela moved to the couch. Valerie slid over to make room for her.

"That's better," Angela said, facing Valerie from barely two feet away. "How old are you, Valerie?"

"Sixteen."

"Sixteen," Angela said. "I have a daughter who's seventeen. She's a lot like you. A pretty girl. Really good at sports."

"What's her name?" Valerie asked.

"Penelope. She hates that name. Insists everybody call her Penny. She says Penelope is a clown's name."

A faint trace of a smile came across Valerie's face.

"She's like you in another way too. When she's got something bothering her, it's really hard for her to talk about it. She bottles things up inside her."

Valerie looked away from Angela.

"Valerie, honey," Angela said. "I want you to look at me. Look right in my eyes."

Valerie turned her head back.

"And I want to hold your hands. Is that okay?"

Valerie nodded as Angela's hands enveloped hers.

"Keep looking at me, honey. I know you have something terrible inside you. The only way things are gonna get better is if you let it out."

Valerie shook her head.

"Valerie, you're safe now. Whatever's hurting you or making you afraid, you can make it stop," Angela said as she brushed aside a strand of hair that had fallen across the girl's face.

"I can't," Valerie whispered in a soft, almost childlike voice.

"Yes, you can, honey. You don't have to be

afraid anymore. You're safe now. You're safe."

Valerie's breathing became faster as tears filled both eyes.

"It's okay, honey. You're safe."

"He's raping me!" Valerie screamed, and began to convulse in sobs as she fell into Angela's embrace.

75

Aline hurried past the patio, through her backyard and around the hedges to Marge's property. It was an unusually cool, cloudy evening, and the sun was just disappearing below the horizon.

Aline could see the light on in the upstairs room that she knew was Jamie's. Through an open window she could hear the audio from a program he was watching. She rang the doorbell, waited, but got no response.

Walking back into the yard she shouted up to Jamie's room. He appeared at the window and said she could come up.

As Aline ascended the stairs, she tried to remember that last time she had babysat her special neighbor. Almost ten years ago, she thought.

The force of Aline's knocks on Jamie's door was enough to open it. He was lying on his bed, staring at the ceiling. The TV was off now. As she looked at Jamie, it was clear that he had been crying.

"My mom's in the hospital," he said. "She went in the ambulance. She's gonna die and go to Heaven with my dad."

Aline sat on the edge of the bed. "Jamie, a lot of people who go to the hospital get better, and they come home. We have to hope and pray that your mom gets better, and that everything will be okay."

"Mom is in the hospital because I'm bad. I'm going to jail, because I did a bad thing. I went swimming with Kerry."

Tears began streaming down Jamie's face. His body shook as he cried softly.

Oh my God, Aline thought. He doesn't even understand what they think he did.

Aline ran her hands up and down his arms. Jamie's long, strong arms reached up and enveloped her in a hug. It was tight, almost painfully so. Despite what he was saying, she could not believe this gentle creature could have hurt Kerry. Was this an opportunity to find out what really happened to her sister?

After giving him a moment or two to calm down, Aline stood up and went over to the window. The lights in her backyard had just come on and illuminated the murky twilight.

Her mind returned to a psychology course she had taken in college. A particularly interesting lecture dealt with the strategy of having child victims reenact the traumas they had undergone as a way to cope with and master them. Was the night of Kerry's death a traumatic experience for Jamie? Had anyone asked him to relate what happened in a way that would allow him to tell the story?

"Jamie, have you had dinner yet?"

"No."

"Is Chinese food still your favorite?"

"Sesame chicken, white rice and wonton soup," Jamie said, a smile returning to his face.

"Okay, I'm going to order Chinese food for you after we play a little game. We're going to pretend it's the night of Kerry's party."

They began with Jamie looking out the back window. "Kerry had a party," he said. "Everybody went home and Kerry was by herself."

"So Kerry was alone. What was she doing?"

"She was cleaning up. Then Alan Crowley came over. He likes Kerry. He kissed her and hugged her."

Pointing to her backyard, Aline asked, "Where did Alan come from?"

Jamie seemed confused by the questions.

Aline took his hand. "Come on. We're going over to my yard. I want you to show me everything you did that night and everything you saw."

76

For the full minute that Valerie cried, Angela held on as the girl buried her head in her shoulder.

"Who is it, Valerie?" Angela asked. "Who did this to you?"

"I can't tell. I told Kerry and she's dead. It's my fault."

Her voice had reached a crescendo of fear and grief. Angela began rocking her. "Valerie, Valerie, you're safe, honey. You're safe."

Marina and Wayne had heard her screaming "He's raping me!" and rushed into the room. "Valerie, Valerie!" Marina cried.

Mike was staring at Wayne. Aline had told him that Valerie seemed to resent her stepfather. Was he the one doing this to her?

As Wayne rushed to Valerie, Mike sprang up. Wayne dropped to his knees beside the couch. "Valerie, baby, tell us who did this to you. You need to tell us."

"It's, it's, my coach, Scott Kimball. He did it. He won't stop."

"The coach," Marina exclaimed. "My God, we let him come in here this afternoon. He was so concerned about Valerie. We even let him talk to her alone."

"He warned me not to say anything to anybody. He said, 'Aline should remember what happened to Kerry,' " Valerie sobbed.

Wayne stood up. "I'll kill him," he said, his voice deadly quiet.

Mike was as dumbfounded as the others. Scott Kimball must have somehow found out that Valerie had confided in Kerry. He took out his cell phone, went to *Contacts* and tapped Aline's cell number. She didn't pick up. Is she in trouble? "I have to check on Aline," he said abruptly.

"Go," Angela said. "I've got things covered here."

He rushed out of the room, ran out the door and to his car. As he was driving he called the Saddle River Police. "Send units immediately to the Chapman house, 15 Waverly Road. Scott Kimball, white male, early thirties, a rapist, and probably a murderer, might be there."

77

They walked downstairs, out the back door and across the lawn. As they entered the Dowling property, Jamie stopped. He bent his head down and started walking around, looking at the grass.

"Jamie, what are you doing?"

"It's not here," he said.

"What's not here?" Aline asked.

"The golf club. It was on the grass."

"Wait here, Jamie."

Aline sprinted around to the garage, grabbed a club, brought it back to where Jamie was standing and handed it to him.

"It was here," he said, putting the club in the grass, and then picking it back up. "I wanted to help Kerry clean up."

"Show me what you did with it."

Jamie picked up the club and carried it over to the pool area. Looking at the end of the club, he said, "This one is clean. The other one was dirty." He put it on top of a recliner at the side of the pool.

So when Jamie picked up the club off the lawn and brought it to the pool area, he believed he was helping to clean up, Aline thought. That explains why his fingerprints are on the murder weapon.

She followed closely behind him. They were facing the patio.

"You're doing a great job, Jamie. Did Alan come back after the party to see Kerry?"

"Yes."

"Show me what he did, where he came from."

Jamie walked to the side of the house, out of her sight.

Then he turned around and came back. He picked up the club off the recliner and laid it on the stone patio. "Alan did this," Jamie said as he picked it up again and leaned it against a patio chair.

"Then what did Alan do?" Aline asked quietly. "Make believe I'm Kerry. Do everything Alan did."

Jamie walked over to her. He gave her a hug, then kissed her forehead. He then walked away and around the side of the house.

When Jamie came back, Aline said, "We are still playing the pretend game. I want you to pretend that I'm Kerry. Now show me what the Big Guy did. Show me where he came from."

Jamie walked to the other side of the backyard that bordered the woods.

Aline felt her phone vibrate in her pocket. She pulled it out and glanced at the name on the screen. "Mike Wilson." She was making progress with Jamie and didn't want to stop. I'll call him back, she thought.

Jamie began tiptoeing across the backyard. As he approached the patio, he motioned Aline to stand closer to the pool.

"Turn around," he said. Aline faced away from Jamie but glanced back over her shoulder at him. Jamie picked up the putter that was leaning against the chair. As he came closer to her he raised the putter high over his head and began to swing it.

"Okay, Jamie, that's enough," Aline said as she raised her hands to protect herself.

"That's what Big Guy did."

"So the Big Guy came out of the woods. He picked up the club and hit Kerry. Then what did he do?"

Jamie nodded as he threw the club into the grass past the pool.

Forcing the words from her lips, Aline asked, "Jamie, are you the Big Guy who hit Kerry?"

Jamie seemed bewildered by the question.

He shook his head, looked all around and when he glanced over at the woods, his expression changed. Pointing emphatically, he yelled, "Aline, he did it. He hit her. Big Guy pushed her in the water."

78

Mike sped down Chestnut Ridge Road and turned onto Waverly Road. Instinct told him not to turn on the siren. If Kimball was with Aline, Mike did not want him to have advance warning of his arrival.

He pulled into the Chapman driveway, sprinted the twenty yards to the front door and rang the bell. While waiting, he slipped the safety off his sidearm holster.

"Come on, Aline, answer," he said out loud as he rang again and pounded on the door with an open hand.

79

Aline was stunned at the sight of Scott Kimball. He was walking toward them, a pistol pointed at them. His smile was a twisted grimace. He began to laugh.

He looked at Jamie. "One day after lacrosse practice you told me your dad called you Big Guy. I told you that's what my dad called me."

Stunned, Aline cried, "Scott, what are you doing here? Are you crazy?"

"No, you are, Aline," he said. "Same as Kerry. Pumping Valerie to tell you things that are none of your business." He laughed loudly. "What is it about you and Kerry that people talk to you when they should keep their mouths shut? I could tell last month that Valerie was getting harder to control. It was only a matter of time before she talked to somebody. I had a feeling that *somebody* was going to be your sister Kerry. I put a tracking device on Kerry's car. It's still on there, by the way, on the car you're driving. That's how I know you went to see Valerie this morning. But let's get back to Kerry. That Saturday morning when Kerry picked up Valerie, I followed the signal to the diner. They got a window seat. The same one you sat in when you showed the waitress the pictures. I couldn't hear what Kerry and Valerie were saying, but from watching I could tell that Valerie was spilling the beans to her."

Aline shrieked, "You killed Kerry! Why?"

"It's Valerie's fault. She came on to me."

"But why did you kill Kerry?"

"Aline, I had to. Valerie was easy to control. Kerry, no chance. Lucky for me, I got wind of Kerry's little beer bash. I waited for an hour in the woods over there, until Kerry was alone. I was about to make an appearance when who comes around the corner but Kerry's Romeo, Alan Crowley."

"He gave Kerry a hug and a kiss," Jamie said.

"I know he did, Jamie. I was watching. But what I hadn't figured on, and this is very bad news for you, Jamie, is that you also were watching —"

Aline interrupted, "You're a coward, Scott. You crept up on my sister and —"

"Oh, that wasn't the plan, Aline. I had

351

every intention of shooting her. But when Alan Crowley brought that golf club over to the patio and then took off, let's just say I improvised."

Aline was trying to think of any way she could to keep him talking. She thought of the call she hadn't taken from Mike. I've got to keep stalling until he gets here.

Scott was coming closer to them.

"Scott, you don't have to do this," Aline pleaded.

"Oh, yes, I do, Aline. With you out of the picture, you and your friend Jamie, Valerie will keep her mouth shut. Just like last time."

80

Maybe she brought Jamie back to her house, Mike thought. He started toward his car but then remembered that a quick cut through the backyards would get him there faster. As he started around the side of the Chapman house, he saw that the lights were on in the Dowling backyard. He heaved a sigh of relief when he saw Aline and Jamie standing by the pool. He was about to call out to her, but he stopped. She wasn't talking to Jamie. Instead they were both looking toward the wooded area that bordered the property. Aline was standing in front of Jamie as if to protect him.

Mike moved quietly across the Chapman rear yard and made his way to the row of hedges that separated the properties. He could see a man approaching them with a gun in his hand. The wail of faraway police sirens began.

Mike pulled out his pistol, put his left

hand under his right fist and assumed a firing stance.

"Kimball," he yelled. "Freeze! Drop the gun!"

Scott swerved in the direction of Mike's voice. Aline turned, pushed Jamie to the ground and sprawled protectively on top of him.

Scott swung his arm holding the pistol back toward Aline and fired. The shot passed inches over her head.

Mike's first shot hit Scott in his left shoulder. He slumped momentarily, then raised his hand with the gun and fired wildly. Mike's next shot shattered two of Scott's ribs, knocking him over backward as his pistol went skidding across the patio.

Mike raced across the lawn to the patio, his pistol still trained on Scott, who was writhing on the ground. From the front of the Chapman house he could hear screeching sirens, the squeal of tires, car doors slamming.

"Back here!" he yelled to the officers, who came running around the house. Holding up his badge while pointing to Kimball on the ground, he said, "Get him an ambulance and arrest him."

Aline was helping Jamie to his feet.

"Were you hit?" Mike yelled as he rushed

to them.

Without answering, Aline threw her arms around Mike.

"Big Guy tried to shoot us," Jamie yelled. "That wasn't very nice."

"Thank God you're both okay," Mike said as he held her.

"You're not getting out of having dinner with me," Aline whispered. "Change of plans. We're having Chinese food with Jamie."

81

Marge was lying quietly in the intensive care unit of the hospital. Cardiogram leads on her chest were monitoring her heart.

The operation had been successful. The grogginess from the anesthesia was wearing off. Her intense worry about Jamie was returning in full measure.

There was a tap on the door and Father Frank walked in. "How are you doing, Marge?"

"It's hard to tell, but I guess okay."

"Well, I have some news that will make you feel a whole lot better. Jamie is home having Chinese food with Aline. She said she'll stay overnight with him at your house tonight."

Father Frank decided to skip the fact that shots had been fired at Aline and Jamie. Instead he began, "The police arrested Scott Kimball, the lacrosse coach at the high school. They are one hundred percent certain that he's the one who murdered Kerry Dowling. It turns out that he's 'the Big Guy' Jamie was talking about."

It took a full minute before the implications of what she had been told sank in. "Oh, thanks be to God," Marge said fervently. "Thanks be to God and his blessed mother!"

82

Alan was sitting with his mother and father in the den. It seemed to him that ever since they'd heard about Jamie's potential involvement in Kerry's murder, they could not stop watching the local news. A breaking story caught their attention. A woman reporter was standing in front of the high school. "Saddle River, New Jersey, high school lacrosse coach Scott Kimball has been arrested for the murder of Kerry Dowling."

Impossible, Alan thought. It's not going to be true.

But it was. In total shock he listened as the details of Kimball's attempted murders of Aline and Jamie were reported. As his mother screamed in relief, tears welled in his eyes. "I can't believe it's really over," he said, "for Jamie and for me. I guess I'll be going to Princeton after all."

83

Fran and Steve were having a quiet dinner at the Bermuda Hamilton Princess. They were the only ones in their corner of the restaurant. At the same time both of their cell phones signaled the arrival of a text. It was from Aline. *Watch this and call me right away!!!!!!!!!!!!*

Puzzled, Fran came around and sat next to Steve. He tapped on the link and the broadcast of the CBS local news began with the arrest of Scott Kimball for the murder of Kerry Dowling and that Aline had saved Jamie's life as Kimball had tried to kill them too.

Fran and Steve fell into each other's arms as they realized that they might have lost their other daughter.

"Fran, Fran," Steve said, his voice husky with emotion, "to think what could have happened."

Fran, filled with relief and overwhelmed

with gratitude, was finding it hard to speak. Then she whispered, "Let's go home. I need to put my arms around Aline."

EPILOGUE

Three Months Later

Scott Kimball had been arraigned while in his hospital bed recovering from his wounds. The charges were the murder of Kerry Dowling, the attempted murders of Aline Dowling and Jamie Chapman, possession of a firearm for an unlawful purpose, and aggravated sexual assault against Valerie Long.

The prosecutor had told Valerie and her parents that there was overwhelming evidence on the other charges and that Kimball would spend the rest of his life in prison. She would not have to testify unless she really wanted to.

Valerie agreed to her parents' suggestion that she go for therapy to help her cope with what Scott Kimball had done to her and the many personal losses she had suffered. She remembered vividly Wayne's furious reaction when he heard what Kimball had done to her. For the first time she viewed him as her father.

Two stents in her heart improved Marge's health considerably. But she insisted that knowing the cloud had been lifted from over Jamie's head was the only medicine she really needed.

Jamie was thrilled that the manager at Acme had offered him his job back. In response to Marge's vehement insistence, it was agreed he would even be given a raise.

Princeton immediately reinstated Alan for the January semester. He was counting the days until he could leave for school. Three months earlier he had no idea what career he wanted to pursue. Now he was pretty sure he wanted to be a defense lawyer.

He was working five nights a week as Christmas help at Nordstrom's. June had found him the job.

Aline and Mike knew the moment they embraced after the shooting that they were destined to hold on to each other forever. They decided they would be married in the fall, after Kerry's one-year anniversary. Fran and Steve would always deeply grieve Kerry's loss, but they were delighted that Aline and Mike would be together. Fran's mind leapt to the future as she thought of holding a grandchild in her arms.

Father Frank would preside at the wedding. Mike's parents loved Aline and could not have been happier with their son's choice.

Father Frank had shared with Aline, Mike, Fran and Steve something Rose Kennedy once said: *"Birds sing after a storm. Why shouldn't people feel as free to delight in whatever sunlight remains to them?"*

ABOUT THE AUTHOR

The #1 *New York Times* bestselling author **Mary Higgins Clark** has written thirty-seven suspense novels, four collections of short stories, a historical novel, a memoir, and two children's books. With her daughter Carol Higgins Clark, she has coauthored five more suspense novels, and also wrote *The Cinderella Murder, All Dressed in White, The Sleeping Beauty Killer,* and *Every Breath You Take* with bestselling author Alafair Burke. More than one hundred million copies of her books are in print in the United States alone. Her books are international bestsellers.